THE
COLOUR
OF
THE
SUN

David Almond

HODDER CHILDREN'S BOOKS
First published in Great Britain in 2018 by Hodder and Stoughton
This paperback edition published 2019

3 5 7 9 10 8 6 4

A CIP catalogue record for this book is available from the British Library.

ISBN 978 1 444 94113 5

Typeset in Bembo by Avon DataSet Ltd, Bidford on Avon, Warwickshire

Printed and bound in Great Britain by
Clays Ltd, Elcograf S.p.A.

The paper and board used in this book
are made from wood from responsible sources.

Hodder Children's Books
An imprint of Hachette Children's Group
Part of Hodder and Stoughton
Carmelite House
50 Victoria Embankment
London EC4Y 0DZ

An Hachette UK Company
www.hachette.co.uk

www.hachettechildrens.co.uk

For Julia

ONE

It's an ordinary summer day, the day that Jimmy Killen dies and comes to life again. It's the middle of the holidays, when it sometimes seems like time stands still, when it seems there's nothing at all to do. Davie's in his bed, in the shadows behind his bedroom curtains when it all begins. The whole day lies before him but he wants to stay there. He wants to be older so he could be with a lass or go drinking with the lads. He wants to be younger so he could run about yelling like a daft thing.

His mam calls up from down below.

'Davie! Get yourself out into the sun, lad!'

He peeps through the curtains. He's dazzled by the light. He can see nothing when he turns back to his room. He rubs his eyes till his sight returns and he sees it all anew.

'Davie!'

'Yes, Mam!'

He starts digging through some ancient toys. Animal masks have been hanging inside his wardrobe door for so long he's nearly forgotten that they're there at all. They've been gathering dust since he was four or five. A gorilla, a tiger, a horse, a fox. The fox was best. He'd pull it on and leap and screech to make his parents terrified. He does it again now, alone in his shady bedroom. He looks out through the fox eyes and raises his claws and he snarls and imagines he's slaughtering a coop full of chickens.

'Davie! What the heck you doing up there?'

He laughs and rips the mask off. He laughs again to see the plastic antlers dangling on the door as well. How could he have forgotten them? He sticks them on his head. He steps quietly through the room, looking out for predators. He rocks his head and shakes the antlers. He leaps and dances silently and soon the antlers start to feel like proper antlers. The room feels like a wood. He starts to lose himself in the old game of being a boy who's also a beast.

He pauses. Why is he doing all this? he wonders.

Maybe it's time to get rid of things, time to chuck

this childish stuff out.

Mam calls from down below again.

'Davie!'

'Aye!' he calls. 'Coming, Mam!'

But he keeps on digging. He finds some ancient colouring pencils, from when he was maybe five or six. There's an old sketch book as well, with a faded green cover and brittle pages. He opens it and comes upon things he hasn't seen for years: scrawled pictures of dark monsters and slithery snakes. Stick figures of his mam and dad, pictures of the house, a scribbly sketch of a lovely black-and-brown dog they used to have called Stew. A page full of pictures of himself. A picture of a baby with messy writing beside it: *Davie as a bayby*. A picture of an ancient man with a beard: *Davie wen he is old*. And here's the beginning of an ancient tale that starts and then gets nowhere past the first two sentences: *Wons ther was a boy calld Davie and he wonted an advencha. So he got sum sanwichs and he got his nife and set owt into the darknes.* The ends of the pencils are chewed and he chews them again and he thinks how weird it is that he's probably tasting himself as he was all those years ago.

'Davie!'

There's an old grey haversack. His dad gave it to him a few years ago. Davie used to stride around the house with it on his back, marching and saluting and carrying an imaginary rifle on his shoulder. He puts the fox mask, the antlers, the pencils and the book into it. He slings it across his shoulders and goes down.

Mam's in the red-hot kitchen. She's been baking, making bara brith and lemon meringue pie, such lovely things. There's a smell of lemon, raisins, warm yeasty dough. Davie salivates as he imagines the delicious food on his tongue.

She stands there with her arms folded. There's drifts of white flour on her red-and-white apron. Dad's favourite painting, of sunflowers, is shining bright on the wall behind her. Sunlight pours into the room.

'About time!' she says. 'Now eat that breakfast and shift those bones.'

She guides him to a chair at the table. There's a bowl of cornflakes and some toast and some orange juice. She hums a tune and spreads her arms and shifts her feet in a gentle dance. She smiles and sighs as he eats and drinks.

'Now get yourself out into the world,' she says.

'What world?'

'The lovely world outside that door.'

He grins.

'I've been there before, Mam. I've seen it all before.'

She grins back at him.

'Aye,' she says. 'But you haven't been in it on this day, and you haven't seen it in this light.'

'And what if there's a mad axeman on the loose out there?'

She taps her cheek and ponders for a moment.

'That's a good point,' she says. Then she shrugs. 'It's just a risk you'll have to take!'

She laughs at the haversack. She asks what's inside and he tells her.

'Those old things!' she says. 'Didn't you use to love them!'

She smiles as she gazes back into the past for a moment.

Then she puts a little package into his hand. It's a piece of warm bara brith, wrapped in greaseproof paper.

'There's butter on it,' she says. 'And there's a slice of Cheshire cheese with it. Won't it be delicious? Put it in the bottom of your sack so you won't be tempted to eat it too soon.'

He does that.

She puts her hands around his head and plants a kiss at the top of his skull. She blows away the floury dust that she leaves there. She spreads her hand across his back, and gently guides him to the door.

'Go on,' she says. 'There'll be time enough for sitting about when you get to be as old as me.'

'I'll never get as old as that!'

'I'm glad to hear it,' she whispers.

She kisses him again.

'Now, my Davie, out you go. Don't hurry back. The day is long, the world is wide, you're young and free.'

And out he goes, to start his wandering.

TWO

Should he go up, he wonders, or should he go down?
He tosses a coin. Down. He doesn't walk far, just to
the heart of this little town, the place he's lived since
he was born, the place where everything is so familiar.

He sits on the grey pavement opposite the houses
on Ethel Terrace, with his back against the wall of the
Columba Club. It's clean enough. No dog muck, no
fag ends, just some dust and slivers of slate that must've
come down from cracks in the roof. Nothing seems to
move. His mood declines. He gets that feeling that he
sometimes gets these days, that he hates this dead-end
place, where nothing seems to happen, nothing seems
to change. Sometimes he just wants to walk out of it
and keep on walking and leave it all behind. But he
knows he's too young to do that yet, and anyway today

7

it's like he's got no energy. Like there's nothing in the world he wants to do.

So he just sits there, in the dust.

For a moment he thinks about Elizabeth McErlane. He met her in the square yesterday evening. She wanted him to go down to Holly Hill Park with her but he held back. She asked if he was daft. She said most lads would be with her like a shot if she asked them to Holly Hill Park.

'You're like a wet weekend,' she said. 'It's like you're on the point of tears even when a lass is making eyes at you.'

He knows she's got a point, but you'd think she'd try to sympathise. She's not the one that lost her dad just a few weeks back. How would she feel about that?

He moves his thoughts away from her. If he's honest, he's not too bothered. He's still more interested in playing football than in being with lasses. He does try, like lots of the lads do, and sometimes he loves it, like lots of the lads do, but kissing's never as sweet as making a perfect diving header or curving the ball into an imaginary net. He has to admit that Elizabeth's very bonny, though, and she does bring about some pretty amazing dreams.

He's in full sunlight. The wall at his back is already warming up. There's hardly a soul in sight. Not a breath of wind. There's somebody singing somewhere far away, and somebody playing a fiddle. As Davie listens, he takes out the sketch book and pencils. He starts to draw what he can see: the dark roadway, the grey pavements, the steel fences and stone walls of Ethel Terrace. It's all so colourless, all so static, all so empty, all so drab. A crow flaps over him and lands on the roof of Ethel Terrace. He draws it, that beautiful streamlined jet-black shape. It stays a few short moments, then it caws and up it goes, black silhouette flying over him, rising into the endless blue. He draws its flight as a black line fading as it stretches to the page's edge. Then closes his eyes and lifts his arms and stretches them out wide at his side. He laughs at himself. Sees himself as Jesus hanging on the cross in agony in church. Then changes what he sees and feels, and has the better feeling, the old feeling he's had since he was small, that his arms are wings. He stretches them wide, becomes a bird, rising from this dry and dusty place, soaring away into the sunlit distance.

'Flying far?' says someone.

Davie comes back to earth and opens his eyes. It's

Wilf Pew from Wellington Street, standing just a few feet away.

'Flying far, I said,' says Wilf.

Wilf's got his long grey coat on even in this heat. He always wears the thing. Maybe he thinks it'll hide the fact that he's got a false leg. Doesn't work. Everybody knows and nobody's bothered. Why should they be?

'Cat got your tongue?' says Wilf.

'No,' says Davie.

'Good.'

Wilf takes a tube of fruit gums out of his pocket and holds it out. There's grey fluff on the orange sweet that's at the top of the tube.

'No, thanks,' says Davie.

Wilf shakes his head in disappointment.

'You young'ns,' he says. 'You should never turn down a gift, you know. What the hell's become of you all?'

He holds the orange fruit gum up to the sun then puts it into his mouth, chews and grins.

'Blimmin' lovely!' he says. 'Absolutely blimmin' lovely!'

He wipes his lips with the back of his hand.

'Anyway,' he says. 'Enough of that. So what's the plan?'

'The plan?'

'Aye, the plan. What you up to? Where you going? How you gonna make yer mark?'

Davie sighs, sits there, says nothing.

'Look at ye,' says Wilf. 'Sitting there with yer face trippin' ye.'

He leans over towards the boy and widens his eyes.

'It might never happen, ye knaa,' says Wilf.

Davie groans. Why do blokes say things like that? What you supposed to say to things as daft as that?

Then Wilf frowns and bends down and bangs himself hard on the thigh of what must be his false leg.

'Damn thing!' he says. 'Be better off without the silly thing. Wouldn't I?'

Davie says nothing.

'The answer is I would!' Wilf snaps. 'One day I'll rip it off and fling it aside and I'll be free!'

Then he starts to limp away and he kind of shimmers in the heat, but he pauses and turns back for a moment.

'I knaa you've had some bother,' he says. 'But there's many a body worse off than you!'

He opens his coat wide and shows his legs.

'This is a world of wonder!' he yells. 'And some folk stroll through it with their eyes down to the dirt like it's all nowt but a great big bore!'

He heads off, but he turns back yet again.

'Look around you!' he says. 'You should be running around dancing and singing your head off at the glory of it all!'

He digs in his pocket and takes out the fruit gums and flings one of the sweets towards Davie. It bounces on the pavement and comes to rest against Davie's leg.

'Eat it up!' says Wilf. 'It'll diy ye good!'

Then he twirls on his false leg and the long grey coat swirls around him. He flinches, and groans in what must be pain, then he giggles at himself and turns his face to the sky and sings a weird, wordless, joyful song.

He yells back one final thing.

'There'll come a time when you have to leave this wondrous place, you know!'

Then at last he's gone.

Davie picks the fruit gum up. It's yellow. He rubs the dust and fluff off it. Wilf Pew. When Davie was a boy he was scared of the bloke, who was always limping back and forward through the town. But Davie's mam told him that Wilf was harmless. She said that one summer he walked all the way to Edinburgh and back just to prove that he could do it. *He's a bold, brave man*, she used to say. And he'd had his dose of tragedy. *Tragedy?* Davie asked. *Aye, the story is he had a lovely lass once and he was about to marry her, and she went and died, too young.*

Davie licks the fruit gum. He eats it. As it dissolves deliciously on his tongue, he shuts his eyes and lets the sun shine down on him. What a summer it's turning out to be. He hears some kids laughing in the park. He sees bonny Elizabeth wandering inside him. He sees his dad sitting on the sofa at home all shrunken and knackered and gasping for breath. He sees other things he doesn't want to see. Why do they keep on appearing like this? Why can't he turn his mind away from them? What is it about the mind that keeps moving from picture to picture, even to ones that are horrible to see?

Then there's something hot and slobbery on his hands. The tongue of a big dog, licking him. Davie gasps. For a moment he thinks it's the black-and-brown dog called Stew, but of course it's not. Yes, it's black-and-brown, but the pattern's really different, and this dog's far bigger, and it's gasping and grunting, and its tongue is horrible and hot and wet. He tries to shove it off but it won't budge so he stands up and shoves it with his foot. It snarls and bares its teeth and looks like it's going to go for him, but in the end it packs in and slopes off.

Davie doesn't know whether to sit down again or to wander a bit more. He thinks about tossing a coin but he doesn't. He looks about and tries to find something colourful to draw, then suddenly somebody else appears right beside him. It's his mate, Gosh Todd. He stands sideways in front of Davie and looks up and down the street like somebody might be watching or listening. Then he leans in close and whispers,

'I seen a body, Davie.'

'Eh?'

'A *body*.'

'What kind of body?'

'A dead one, Davie. Do you want to see?'

THREE

'It's in the rubble,' says Gosh. 'Where they're pulling down the old church hall.'

He looks Davie in the eye like he's waiting for him to say something but Davie doesn't know what to say.

'Are you sure it was dead?' he says at last.

'Aye. I seen the knife.'

'The knife?'

'Aye. The one that killed him. There was blood and everything, Davie.'

Davie tries cursing and swearing to see if that feels like the right kind of thing to say.

'Whose body was it?' says Davie.

'I can't be sure,' says Gosh. 'I seen it and I nearly jumped out me skin and didn't dare get too close. But I think it was Jimmy Killen.'

'Eh? Why would it be Jimmy Killen?'

'He had them tight jeans on that he wears. And that green checky Levi shirt.'

Davie tries cursing and swearing again.

'Jimmy Killen,' he whispers.

'Aye. And if it was Jimmy Killen then I reckon the killer was Zorro Craig.'

Gosh nods and grins and widens his eyes.

'Aye,' he goes on. 'Zorro Craig. It's obvious when you think about it, isn't it? Who else could it be? It's how it was all bound to turn out.'

'Was it?'

'Aye. You know how they went on. You know how they hated each other, like all the Craigs hate all the Killens and all the Killens hate all the Craigs.'

'I thought that was over and done with.'

'Mebbe it's not that easy. And them two, they were the worst of the lot of them, weren't they? They were like bliddy beasts.'

Gosh is right about the Killens and the Craigs. It's been going on for years, ever since Davie's dad was a kid. His dad never understood it. Davie never understands it. How could two families get into such a state about each other? Why did they not get fed up with hating each other? But could it really come to *this*? *Murder*? Could Zorro Craig really be a murderer? Aye, he was mental. But *this*?

'Anyway,' says Gosh, 'I run down to the police station and I tell the sergeant there. He says am I sure I'm not just seeing things. Like he thinks that nowt like that could happen in a place like this, or like he thinks somebody like Gosh Todd would say anything to get folk stirred up on a sleepy sunny morning. But in the end he knows he has to take a look, 'specially when he realises the Craigs and Killens might be involved, so he goes with me and that's that. He gets the doctor and the priest. They telt me to tell nobody but now I've telt you. Do you wanna come and see?'

Davie hesitates.

'Howay,' says Gosh. 'It was just half an hour ago. Mebbe it'll still be there.'

Davie hesitates. What would it be like to see a body? And to see a body that had been murdered? And Zorro Craig? Everybody knew he was a monster. But would he *kill*?

'Howay,' says Gosh. 'It's not every day you get a chance like this.'

Gosh looks at the pencils and the book.

'And you've got to admit it's a bit more interesting than colouring in.'

Davie shrugs. He has to go, he has to see. He puts the pencils and the book into his sack, puts the sack on his back and off they go.

Of course, lots of folk have heard by now that something's going on down there. As they head across the square and down the High Street there's lots of people doing the same. They're frowning and whispering and shrugging.

One of Davie's neighbours, a woman called Mrs Keen from number six that used to be a teacher, stops him as he and Gosh hurry by.

'What's going on, Davie?' she asks in a trembly voice.

Gosh knocks Davie with his elbow, telling him to tell her nowt.

'I don't know,' Davie tells her. 'Maybe it's just nowt.'

She clicks her tongue.

'Don't say nowt, Davie,' she says. 'It's so coarse. The word is nothing.'

'Sorry, Mrs Keen,' says Davie. 'I know that.'

And they walk on.

The old school hall's through some gates just past

the church. It's been getting demolished for the past month or so. *Good riddance to it*, thinks Davie. Some of the most boring times of his life have happened in there. Prayer meetings and hymn practices and talks about the body and the soul and whether it's a sin to think too much about girls. Unhappy, boring blokes in black telling kids to lift their souls up to the Lord and to tiptoe past the chasms that lead to Hell. God, how he hated all that stuff. Get rid of it all. Cart it away.

There's a fire engine parked up on the High Street. There's a couple of police cars. There's an ambulance inside the gates. There's a massive policeman, PC Poole, standing by the gates telling people to keep back. Folk are talking in hushed voices. Nobody knows anything, but something must have got out because there's whispering about death and murder and mayhem. Davie sees some kids he knows. Shona Doonan's there, in a bright red dress. She's from a family of singers and musicians, the Doonans. They sang some of Davie's dad's favourite songs in the Columba Club after the funeral. 'Waters of Tyne'. 'Felton Lonnen', 'Bonny at Morn'. Maybe it was her that he heard singing. She waves at him.

He waves shyly back. He looks up at the church, that's just a short walk away from here. He blinks, and he sees his dad's coffin being carried in. He sees it being carried out. He sees the funeral cars, all the people dressed in black. He sees himself holding his mam's arm. He sees her holding him.

'Howay, man, Davie.'

Gosh grabs Davie's arm. He guides him through the crowd to PC Poole, who holds his hand out like he's ordering traffic to stop. Gosh stoops under the hand then stands on tiptoe and whispers to the policeman like he whispered to Davie.

'I'm the one that found the body,' he says.

Poole narrows his eyes.

'I'm the one that telt the sergeant about it,' Gosh says. 'It's Jimmy Killen, isn't it?'

Poole says nowt. The crowd's getting bigger. They're pressing at the gate.

The policeman's getting cross.

'Hold your horses!' he snaps at the crowd.

'I'm right, aren't I?' says Gosh.

Davie and Gosh peer past the policeman. Gosh tells Davie that the ambulance is hiding the spot where the body is. Davie leans sideways trying to see but he can't. All he sees is rubble, no body.

'I think I know who might of done it,' says Gosh.

Poole narrows his eyes again.

'Done what?' he says.

'Committed the murder,' says Gosh. 'It is a murder, isn't it?'

Poole says nowt.

'It is,' says Gosh. 'And I know who done it. Me mate does and all.'

Poole looks at Davie. He can feel he's blushing.

'Aye,' says Gosh. 'So mebbe you should let us through so we can have a word with the sergeant.'

Poole looks uncertain.

'Keep back, will you?' he says to the crowd. 'Show a bit of order and respect.'

'You should,' says Gosh. 'The killer could be miles away already.'

'Every minute counts,' says Davie.

He catches his breath. He hadn't expected to say anything at all but he finds he's very pleased with himself.

Gosh is too.

'What Davie says is right,' he says.

'What if he's already tracking down his next victim?' says Davie.

'What if he's already killed again?' says Gosh.

The policeman glances back towards where the invisible sergeant is.

'OK,' he tells the two lads. 'Go through.'

They walk past the ambulance. There's a driver at the wheel reading the *Daily Mirror* and smoking a cigarette, dead calm, like a murder happens every day in these parts. There's a lass sitting beside him who must be a nurse. Behind the ambulance there's the sergeant and old Dr Drummond and daft Father Noone. Davie sees most of the body now: legs in jeans, black winklepicker boots, a green checky Levi shirt. Davie's seen Jimmy walking round wearing that. He'd love one just like it for himself. He starts wondering what'll happen to the shirt now that Jimmy's dead. There's a splash of blood on it, bright red against the green. Davie wonders if the bloodstains will wash off. The priest's kneeling there as well. He's bobbing back and forward as he prays, and between the bobs Davie sees the face. Yes, definitely Jimmy Killen. The priest's got a little crucifix in his hand and he's pressing it on Jimmy's brow and muttering something low and gentle.

Davie stares. He's never seen anybody dead before. His mam said he could go to see his dad in the chapel of rest if he wanted to but he couldn't do it. Jimmy just looks like he did in life, not much different at all.

'It's you,' says the sergeant to Gosh.

'Aye,' says Gosh. 'And this is me mate, Davie.'

'What's he got to do with it all?'

'He knows who the killer is.'

The doctor and sergeant both goggle at Davie.

Davie can't look at them because now he can see the knife, lying on the rubble next to Jimmy's chest. There's blood on it, on the blade and the handle.

'I telt you,' says Gosh.

The priest doesn't stop muttering. His lips are close to Jimmy's ear.

'So who's the killer?' says the doctor.

'Zorro Craig,' Davie finds himself saying.

'Zorro *Craig*!' says the doctor.

'How do you know *that*?' says the sarge.

Davie stares at Jimmy's face again. It's pale and still. It's like Jimmy's just asleep.

The sarge asks Davie again.

'Gosh told me,' says Davie.

'And how do *you* know?' says the sarge.

''Cos Jimmy's a Killen and Zorro is a Craig. They're a bunch of animals and they've always been at war, haven't they? And them two were the worst of all.'

'But we cannot jump to . . .' starts the sarge.

'I heard him saying it when he was six years old,' says Gosh. '"Aa'm ganna kill ye, Killen."'

The doctor and the sergeant stare at Gosh in wonder.

'You heard it and all, didn't you, Davie?' says Gosh.

'Aye,' mutters Davie. 'We were all pretty mental back then.'

'Aye, but it . . . intensified,' says Gosh. 'I heard him just last week in Holly Hill Park. Last Tuesday, it was. "Ye'll get what's comin," he says. "Killen, aa'm ganna send ye to yer grave."'

'Bliddy hell,' says the sarge. 'And why would he say something like that last Tuesday?'

'Dunno,' says Gosh. 'It's what enemies do. I think this time it was something about a lass.'

'About a lass?' says the sarge.

'Aye,' says Gosh. 'It's usually lasses, isn't it? Like in ancient times.'

'*What*?' says the sarge. 'Which lass?'

Gosh shrugs.

'Dunno,' he says.

He turns to Davie.

'Do *you* know?' he says.

'*Me*?' says Davie.

'I think they both had lots of lasses,' says Gosh. 'But mebbe this time it was doomed love.'

Davie looks at Gosh. *What the hell's he on about?*

The doctor mutters something.

'Eh?' says the sarge.

'I said the human condition is a vessel of great mystery,' says the doctor.

'You're right there, doc,' says the sarge.

The priest stops his muttering. He presses his thumb on to Jimmy's brow. He says, 'Amen.'

He stands up and looks like he's come out of some dream. There's grey plaster dust all over his black clothes.

'I have done what I can,' he says. 'I'm sure the lad's sins will be forgiven.' He says the same thing that he said about Davie's dad. 'I'm sure God will have prepared a place for him.'

For Jimmy Killen? Davie wants to say, but he doesn't.

He looks at the air above the body like he expects to see Jimmy's soul floating there, like he expects to see it rising from the demolition site and into the wide clear sky.

The sarge takes a little black notebook and pencil out of his pocket. He opens the book and starts to write then stops. He frowns.

'This is all happening a bit too quick for me,' he says. Tears are gathering in his eyes. His lips are trembling. 'I wish it wasn't happening at all,' he says.

'Strange events can take place anywhere, sergeant,' Davie finds himself saying.

'And who knows what can fester in the human heart?' says Gosh.

Davie stares at him. Where the hell did Gosh learn to say something like that?

The priest steps off the rubble and some of it slips and Jimmy's body lurches sideways. The sergeant gasps in horror. For a moment Davie expects everything, Jimmy's body, rubble and all, to collapse into the dark dingy cellars that he knows exist just below. But it doesn't. Everything settles into place again.

The sergeant blows his breath out.

He looks just like a little boy dressed up in policemen's clothes.

'Top brass from Newcastle are on their way,' he says.

He takes his helmet off and sweat trickles down from his forehead.

'They'll know what to do,' he says.

'They'll probably want to talk to you, lad,' he says to Gosh. 'And mebbe to you as well,' he says to Davie.

Davie looks towards the crowd at the gates. They're dying to get in to see. He waves at Shona again and she waves back. She's really bonny. He'd never properly noticed before.

There's a siren somewhere in the distance.

'That must be them,' says the sarge. 'Thank God for that.'

'What do we do about Jimmy?' says Davie.

'That's not for you to think about,' says the sarge. 'He can't be moved, not till there's instructions from the top.'

The sun's shining bright on Jimmy Killen. It's getting hotter. How soon till a body starts to rot, till it starts to stink? Davie looks past the church and over the rooftops towards the hills at the top of town. It's all a bit stupid. It's like the whole town's come to look at a poor body lying in the dust. He's bored with it already. He wants to get away. He wants to be free. He's thinking of wandering up that way, going up to the top and over the top and carrying on into the sunlit distance all alone. Maybe that's the way that Zorro Craig went after he killed Jimmy, if he did kill Jimmy. It'd make sense. There's so much space over there, so many places to run and hide. Places you could hide for ever if you really wanted to. That's where Davie will head for.

The doctor's holding Gosh's face and looking into his eyes.

'How are you feeling, young man?' he says.

Gosh shrugs.

'Champion,' he says.

'Do you need me?' says Davie to the sarge.

'Need you?'

'To give evidence or anything?'

'Anyone who knew the lad will be questioned, I expect.'

'Can I go?'

'*Go?*' says Gosh. 'Where you bliddy going?'

'Nowhere,' Davie tells him. 'Just wandering.'

'*Wandering?* But, Davie, man.'

Davie shrugs. He knows Gosh won't want to come with him. He'll want to stay here where the excitement is.

'Mebbe I'll catch up with Zorro Craig,' says Davie. 'Mebbe I'll hunt him down and bring him back to justice.'

The sergeant grunts.

'Don't you think of that,' he says. 'That's a job for the professionals, lad.'

The doctor catches Davie's arm as he turns away.

'And you?' he says. 'Are you champion as well, young man?'

Davie doesn't answer. He's known this kind and ancient doctor for as long as he can remember. He can recall the feeling of his fingers as he tapped Davie's chest, the coldness of the stethoscope above his heart, the gentle tap on his cheek, the gentle voice that told his mam she had herself a fine strong little lad. And he can recall the day of his dad's death. The doctor stood in the living room with his black bag in his hand and murmured to Davie's mam that he was so sorry, that there was nothing anybody could have done. Then he opened the door to step out, and Davie saw black-clad Father Noone coming along the street, already heading towards his home.

'Are you?' says the doctor again.

'Aye,' Davie says. 'I'm champion, Dr Drummond, thanks.'

He walks off.

'Don't put yourself in harm's way,' says the doctor.

Davie keeps on walking. It's like he's being lifted out of himself, like he's coming to life.

FOUR

As he passes PC Poole and twists his way through the crowd, folk keep trying to get the answers from him.

'Is it true?' some of them say.

'Is what true?'

'That there's a body? That there's been a murder?'

Davie says he can't say nowt.

They name some names and one or two of them even name Jimmy Killen but Davie's face doesn't flicker.

'A murder!' someone gasps. 'Here, in Little Felling!'

'The telly'll be here. All the papers!'

'It happens, even in places like this.'

'Why shouldn't it happen here? The world is a strange and wicked place.'

Davie keeps on moving.

'Is it true?' they keep on asking.

'The world is weird,' Davie says. 'And who knows what festers in the human heart?'

He passes close to Shona. She touches his arm and comes in close.

Her red dress is bright as fire in the sunlight.

'Did you see it?' she says.

'See what?'

'The body, Davie! You did, didn't you?'

'Aye,' he answers.

'What was it like? Was it scary? Could you look upon it?'

She's got such a sweet and lovely voice, like she's singing even when she's talking, even when she's asking about things like this.

'Was it you singing?' he asks her.

'When?'

'Just this morning. Just a little while ago.'

'I'm always singing, Davie.'

She shrugs.

'So it could have been,' she says.

His mind goes back to the Columba Club, after the funeral, when the guests were leaving. He'd asked her how the hell she could sing so well.

She'd shrugged and smiled.

'It just pours out of me, Davie,' she said. 'It just pours out of all of us, the way that songs pour out of birds.'

She touched his arm.

'I'm so sorry about your dad,' she said.

He'd thanked her for that.

'It could pour out of anyone,' she said as he turned back to his mam. 'It could pour out of you, Davie, if you found a way to let it.'

She's so lovely. Her blue eyes are so bright. He tells her the body was strange, that it was amazing, that it seemed to be only sleeping, still alive. She listens, and he imagines staying here with her, watching everything along with her, then walking away from this place with her at dusk, holding her hand, going far into the distance, filled with excitement, but he tells himself he must keep moving.

'I've got to go, Shona,' he says.

'I could come with you,' she says softly. 'If you'd like me to.'

He almost says yes but he says no.

'I'm not even sure where I'm going,' he says.

'Ah, well. Mebbe we'll see each other when you get back.'

'Aye. I hope so.'

He walks away.

Mrs Keen's there, hovering. She's on tiptoes and her eyes are wide and scared and excited.

'What is the truth, Davie?' she says as he passes by.

Davie shrugs.

'I can't say nowt, Mrs Keen.'

She's about to say something back, but suddenly there's screaming and sobbing and here's Jimmy Killen's mother with a policewoman coming down the High Street.

'Jimmy!' she sobs as the policewoman guides her towards the crowd and towards her dead son beyond. 'Jimmy! My little Jimmy!'

So that's it. The truth is out.

And now here's the top brass from Newcastle, big blokes in black uniforms, squashed into a little blue police car with a blue light flashing on its roof.

Davie heads up the High Street past all the shops. Everybody else is streaming down. Shopkeepers are gathering together in their doorways, gossiping. Jack Hall the newsagent is clambering about in his front window, putting stuff in a rack: American cop magazines, murder mysteries, Batman comics. Joe Wiffen's writing in white on his window: *Brown Ale and McEwans Export at Nockdown Prices Ask Inside.*

Already some of the shops are shut and the owners are heading to the murder scene.

Davie's suddenly hungry. Luckily, Molly Myers hasn't closed the pork shop doors.

Davie goes inside and buys a pork pie.

'You been down there, son?' Molly asks.

'Aye,' says Davie.

'What's the info? Any clues?'

He may as well tell her now.

'Jimmy Killen's been killed,' he says.

'Jimmy *Killen*?'

'Aye. He's been knifed, Mrs Myers.'

'Hell's teeth. Who by?'

He can't tell her that. He bites into the pork pie. It's delicious, the way the meat and the jelly around it mix with the pastry, the way it clags together in his mouth.

'I dunno,' he says.

He takes another bite. He checks his change and tries to buy another pie but Molly says he can have it for nowt. She holds it out to Davie and bows her head like it's an offering.

'That's for the info,' she says. 'Jimmy Killen, eh?'

'Aye.'

'I know how crazy that lot get. But *this*?'

She shakes her head.

'What's the world coming to?' she says.

Davie shakes his head.

'Dunno,' he says. 'It's all a mystery, Mrs Myers.'

She smiles.

'It is that,' she answers.

As Davie turns away she asks him.

'Where you going?'

'I'm not sure, Mrs Myers.'

'Is it safe?'

'Safe?'

'Is it safe to be wandering off when there's a murderer in town?'

'But he could be anywhere, Mrs Myers.' He looks to the back of the shop, where the massive meat fridge is. 'He could be hiding in your meat fridge, Mrs Myers.'

She gasps and her eyes widen in shock.

'In me meat fridge?'

He can see she's trembling.

'Shall I have a look?' he says.

'Aye. Take this knife, though, eh?'

She puts a long butcher's knife into his hand. He goes to the fridge door. He knows the murderer probably won't be in there but he feels his heart thudding. Mrs Myers is gasping. His hand trembles as he reaches for the handle. He doesn't know whether to ease it open dead slowly so that the murderer suspects nothing, or to yank it open suddenly in order to terrify him. And he doesn't know what he'll do if he does find the killer in there. Will he go wild and attack Zorro with the knife? Will he turn around and run out of the shop howling? Will he just stand there and scream in terror? In the end he slowly inches the door open. He raises the knife in preparation but then he lowers it again. Nothing. The fridge is big enough for one or two murderers to be hiding in it. But all that's inside is a single dead skinned pig hanging from a hook.

'Nothing,' he says to Mrs Myers.

'Nothing,' she sighs. 'Oh, thank you, son.'

She puts her hand out for the knife. For a moment he wonders if he should borrow it, and keep it in his sack, in case he needs it during the day. But she takes it from him.

'You be careful as you go on,' she says.

'I will be, Mrs Myers.'

He goes out again with the two pies in his hand. He finds himself thinking about the dead pig in the fridge and the dead pig in the pies. Once, in the church hall, he was with a group of kids talking with a visiting priest about animals and souls. Patricia Knott asked if animals had souls the way that people do. She said she was sure her cat had a soul. The cat was called George. She said she could see the soul shining through George's eyes. She said it looked almost human. The priest glared. He said that Patricia was wrong. He told her she must not think in that way. It was heresy. Beasts are not spiritual beings. They are lesser than humans. Only human beings have souls, with all the blessings and the perils that this brings. Only human beings are made in the image of God.

When they left the church hall, Patricia groaned.

'What a load of bollix,' she said.

Davie looks at the inside of the pie. The meat's dull grey and pink with bits of white in it. Fat, he supposes. The jelly's like glue. He takes another bite. If the pig did have a soul, where would the soul be now? Is there a heaven for pigs, he wonders. And if there is, do they run free and wild in it like ancient boars did in ancient forests? Or do they just lie about and sing to God like dead humans are supposed to do? He stops himself. Why's he thinking like this? He stopped believing in

Heaven when he was eight. It sounded like a truly boring place.

Then he finds himself wondering about the pig's blood. What happens to that when a pig's made into pies? He sees the piles of black pudding in Mrs Myers' window. Aye, of course, that's what blood turns into. Makes him feel sick. He's never liked black pudding ever since he discovered what it came from. Not like his granddad. He eats platefuls of the horrible stuff. And white pudding too, which is even more disgusting, 'specially when it's splattered with Hoe's Chutney.

Then he gets to wondering about pigs' bones but he stops that as well. *That's quite enough of that,* he tells himself. *Stop thinking. Stop wondering about everything. Just walk.*

He finishes the first pie as he walks. He puts the other one into his haversack. He heads uphill across the square and on to Felling Bank past the Co-op and Dragone's coffee shop. Dragone's is empty now but pretty soon it'll be full of excited, scared, astonished, gasping people, talking about Jimmy and about murder and death over pots of tea, cups of coffee, ham sandwiches and Dragone's Knickerbocker Specials. Davie licks his lips. Knickerbocker Specials. Ice cream and cold custard and bright-coloured jelly. So delicious.

Eddie Mace is opening the doors of The Bay Horse.

'There'll be many a pint sunk today,' he tells Davie as he passes by.

'Will there?' says Davie.

'Aye, there always is when there's a big event or a special occasion.'

He laughs.

'And you don't get a much bigger occasion than a murder.'

'Don't you?'

'No. Remember the Windy Nook poisoner? Sorry, 'course you don't. Before your time. You're far too young. She killed three husbands with rat poison. There was serious drinking for weeks when the news of that got out.'

He laughs again.

'Aye, those were the days, son.'

Davie walks on. He does know about the poisoner. She lived in a bungalow just down the street from his grandma. Yes, it was before his time, but his granddad told him about it one night after he'd been to The Black House. She seemed a canny little woman, his granddad said. Neat and tidy. Won the WI jam-making competition three years in a row. Had a cheerful hello for everybody. Handed sweets out to children passing her front gate. She buried husband number three in the back garden and planted leeks on top of him. 'Who'd have thought it?' he said. 'Who knows what's going on in someone's heart?'

Davie walks on. No, there's no way of knowing what really goes on in somebody's heart. And there's no way of knowing where a murderer might hide, or which way he went. So you may as well go anywhere. And, anyway, if the killer is Zorro Craig, why would he want to kill anybody else except for a Killen? And Davie isn't Davie Killen.

Suddenly, there's Wilf Pew from Wellington Court again, limping downhill. How the hell did he get here? How come he's always on the move?

'I telt ye, didn't I?' says Wilf. 'There's many a body worse off than you.'

'Is there?' says Davie.

'Yes, there is. You're not blimmin' dead, are you?' He leans towards Davie like he's having a proper look. He pokes him in the chest as if to check he's real. 'At least, I don't think you are!' He laughs. 'Or mebbe you're alive and dead all at the same time.'

Davie rolls his eyes. What's he supposed to say to something like that?

'Mebbe we all are, come to think of it,' says Wilf.

Davie decides not to ask Wilf what he means. He wants to move on.

Wilf holds his fruit gums out. The top one is bright green. Davie doesn't take it.

Wilf lifts it up towards the sky.

'Look at it, man!' he says. 'Look at the sun shining through it and you could take it and put that blazing colour deep inside yourself and you blimmin' hesitate?'

He takes out another, a purple one, and lifts that up too.

'What's wrong with you, lad?' he says. 'Don't you see the blimmin' beauty of it?'

Davie does. He sees how the fruit gum glows at the tip of Wilf's fingers beneath the sun against the vivid blue. Wilf holds it out to him like a priest holding out a communion wafer. Davie shrugs and puts out his hand and Wilf places it on his palm. Davie raises it to his mouth. He feels the fluff on his tongue as he starts to chew, feels the smoothness of the sweet, the lovely gumminess of it.

'Is it good?' says Wilf.

'Aye.'

'Aye. And now it's all inside you, all that purple, all that weird light.'

He pushes the green gum into Davie's hand.

'That one's even lovelier,' he says.

'Thank you.'

'Good lad. Crack on.'

And as quickly as he'd appeared, he's gone.

Davie chews the green gum, mixes it in his mouth with the remnant of the purple gum. It's so sweet, so delicious. He thinks of the multi-coloured light inside himself and the thought pleases him. He cracks on. He continues uphill. He already knows he'll write a story about this day. It'll be called *The Death of Jimmy Killen* or *The Body in the Rubble* or *Blood on a Green Checked Shirt* or *The Soul Within the Pie*. Or maybe he'll call it after something else that'll happen, something he can't possibly know about yet, as the day drifts by.

On he slowly goes, and as he goes he starts to think that maybe he himself is living in a story. *If that was true,* he thinks, *then there'd be no way of knowing it, would there?* All he can do is walk and think that he's the one that decides to do the walking.

He loves wandering uphill like this, away from the

busyness and clutter at the centre. As the fruit gums dissolve to nothing but an aftertaste in his mouth, he thinks of what folk would see if they watched him from below. They'd see the haversack with the things he carries bobbing at his back. They'd see somebody leaving everything behind. They'd see him getting smaller and smaller, and after a while they'd see nothing at all. He'd just be a memory, an after-image.

He thinks of becoming lost, of becoming invisible, of disappearing from the world and becoming nothing at all. He thinks of the world becoming a world without a Davie in it. The world will be as it was before he was born, or as it will be after he's dead. As he's pondering, a voice calls out.

'Now then, Davie!'

He's startled from his thoughts. It's the young priest, Father Kelly. He's on a bench by the pathway, with his ankle-length black cassock draped upon his body and the white collar round his neck, with the bright sun pouring down upon him.

'Hello, Father,' Davie says.

He's a man with a quick laugh and quick feet and a light voice as he traipses through this little town. The people of the parish are fond of him. They look forward to the day he'll take over the parish from daft old Father Noone.

'Come and sit with me a moment, son,' he says. 'And don't call me Father. How can a man like me be any father at all?'

'OK, Father,' says Davie.

They both laugh.

'The name is Paddy,' says the priest. 'Paddy Kelly, from the hills of blessed Kerry.'

FIVE

Davie goes to sit with him.

''Tis a grand bright day in the Kingdom of the Lord,' says Paddy Kelly.

'It is,' says Davie.

The priest raises an eyebrow.

'Is it?' he says. 'The Kingdom of the Lord? What bollix, eh?'

Davie laughs.

'That's a grand word, Davie, don't you think so? *Bollix*?'

'It is,' says Davie.

Davie rolls the word around his mouth. *Bollix*. He likes the feel of it on his tongue and lips and breath, and the sound of it in his mind. It's weird how the words that some folk say you aren't supposed to say can sound like the loveliest words of all. *Nowt. Canny. Howay. Bollix.*

'I'm glad that you agree,' says the priest. '*Bollix.* Better than all that Latin drivel that pours forth from me gob.'

The priest tugs at the white collar around his throat.

'This damn thing,' he mutters.

He leans back on the bench and lets the light of the sun pour down upon him. Davie thinks of moving on but he sits there and lets the light pour down on him as well.

The priest's a handsome man. Davie's mother has told him that. It was he who said the Mass at the funeral. He said that the life of Davie's dad had been a good life. He talked of the deep love between husband and wife. He said that love makes our lives worthwhile. At the graveside real tears flowed from his eyes.

'Sometimes,' he said afterwards in the Columba Club, as the Doonans began their singing and playing, 'we have to wonder what kind of god could take our loved ones from us when they are so young. Sometimes . . .'

Mam waited for the priest to go further, to bring some more explanation or comfort, but the priest just sighed and stopped his words. He turned away and was quickly dancing before the Doonans with his head thrown back and his vestments swirling. He danced all the way until the Doonans' set was done, even when the song was sweet and slow.

'It's the Irish in him,' Davie's mam said. 'They like to lose themselves in it.'

She danced herself, to one of those slow sweet tunes, and Davie knew that she lost herself in the dance too, that she imagined her husband dancing at her side, that she saw him there beside her, brought back to her for a few short moments by the music that he knew and loved so well.

'You're having a walk?' says Father Kelly, opening his eyes.

'Yes, Father. I mean, Yes, Paddy.'

'Good lad. Where you headed?'

Davie shrugs, points uphill.

'Dunno, really.'

'Like the wandering pilgrims, eh?'

Davie shrugs again.

'It's what I loved to do meself, back when I was a lad in County Kerry. Ah, the mountains, Davie, and the sun and the rain, the greenness of the grass beneath

me feet, the yellow in the hedges, the blueness of
the sky above me head, those distant jagged islands
in the blue, blue sea . . . What about the dead lad,
by the way?'

'The dead lad?'

'The one that's down below.'

'Jimmy Killen?'

'Aye, that's the one. Still dead, is he?'

'Aye. I think so, anyway.'

'That's the way of things, I suppose. Despite all the
hopes we might have, eh? They say he was murdered,
don't they?'

'Yes.'

'Ha. We've been killing each other since the start of
time, and where does that get us to?'

'Nowhere.'

'Exactly. Nowhere. Anyway, Kerry. The priests told
us lads that God loved Kerry before any other place
within the world. Maybe they say that about this place.
Have you ever heard it said, that God loves Tyneside
before any other place within the world?'

'No. I don't think I've ever heard anybody saying
that.'

'Nevertheless, it is a grand place, don't you think so?

It is a kind of heaven, don't you think so?'

'Yes, Paddy.'

'Good. And they said that in a bonny place like Kerry, God might look down and speak to good and bonny lads like me. So I grew up thinking that I might hear the voice of the Lord in my little tender lugs. Did you ever think that, Davie?'

'Think what?'

'Did you ever think you might hear God speaking to you, in this bonny place of yours?'

Davie ponders. No, he has never thought so, though he has often thought that there is a presence or a spirit all around him here, that even the stones and the trees and the grass and the air are alive and that they speak to him in some weird way. There's something in the light, the birdsong, the many beauties that are natural to this place, in ordinary little things that sometimes seem miraculous.

'No,' he says. 'I did not.'

'I'm pleased to hear it. Anyway, I must have been about eleven when they asked me, "Has the Lord been speaking to you, little Paddy Kelly, as you wander over this green and past this yellow and below this blue?"'

'And had he?'

'Now that's the thing. I thought he had, Davie! When we're young, every bliddy thing is speaking to us. Don't you find that, Davie? I see you do! And this of course was back in blasted Ireland when God and his priests were everybliddywhere. *Bliddy*. That's another good one. Don't you find that?'

'Yes. *Bliddy* is very fine.'

'So I said, "Yes, I think he has," and they said, "Now this is a grand thing, Paddy Kelly." And they asked me, "What did God say to you?" And you know, Davie, I suddenly realised I didn't have the faintest clue what God had said.'

'So what did you tell them?'

'Ha! I told them that God had asked me to walk with him. I told them that God had said he wished me to be always at his side.'

He's shaking his head and laughing softly but there is torment in his eyes. He tugs again at the white collar around his throat above the black.

'I knew what they wanted, you see,' he says. 'I knew the kind of things God was supposed to say. And it delighted them. They said I had been chosen! And they said, "Now we will take you away from the green and the yellow and the blue and we will show you how to dress in black and turn into the priest that you have been called to be by God himself."'

Davie enjoys the sounds and rhythms of Paddy Kelly's voice. He tries to imagine a joyful lad called Paddy before he was spoken to by God, before he had the vestments on him. It's not too difficult. The young boy still shines through the young man's eyes.

And he imagines taking the black vestments to himself. He imagines them hanging heavy on his body. He feels how they would weigh him down, suffocate him, deaden him.

'I'm in the wrong tale, Davie,' says Paddy.

'The wrong tale?'

'Just look at me. I should be buried in a tale of Darkness, Death and Hell. Should be trudging through some black and gloomy underworld.'

He grunts like a desperate beast. He moans like a ghost.

'It's like I'm as dead as the dead lad down below, Davie,' he says.

He groans and keels over on to the arm of the bench as if he's dead.

'Write me a different tale!' he says. 'Dress me in

bonny clothes and set me dancing up the hill! Bring me to life!'

He laughs. Davie laughs with him.

'OK, Paddy,' he says.

'No need,' says Paddy. 'I've already started it. I'm already writing a new life.'

He looks around. There's no one nearby. He leans a little closer to Davie.

'Have you ever been in love, lad?'

Davie can't answer. The priest smiles.

''Course you haven't,' he says. 'Sorry.'

Father Kelly takes deep breaths. At last he says,

'I think I am in love, Davie.'

The priest unbuttons his white priest's collar. He laughs.

'Ah, the air upon me neck, Davie! Don't you think we live in a grand world, that has such air in it?'

'Yes.'

'Of course you do! This could be Heaven itself. Don't you think that, Davie?'

'Yes.'

'Yes,' he continues. 'That's the thing. I think I am in love.'

Davie looks back at him. He wonders if he should

say something in reply.

'I tell you this,' says the priest, 'because I see myself in you. I am you, wandering these fine streets on a fine Tyneside day. You are me, wandering the hills of Kerry. I'm in love, Davie. That's the top and tail of it, the in and out of it, the beginning and the end of it. I am head over heels, and I think I will not be much longer in these black and heavy clothes. Do I shock you, Davie?'

'No.'

'I won't trouble you with the details of it. But I have fallen in love with a woman from these streets. And she has fallen too. And let me tell you that the voice of Love is stronger than any voice of any god . . .'

He ponders, then he digs into a pocket in his vestments. He takes out a little black prayer book with a thin golden cross on its cover, flicks through its pages and then holds it out to Davie.

'Look at this dreadful little thing,' he says. 'Look at those thin mean lines of tiny black writing. Look at the drivel that is in it.' He bites his lip. 'It's time to cast it out. You're a lad for the books. Mebbe you'd like to carry it now. A relic of the dreadful way things used to be.'

Davie hesitates.

'You could just chuck it into the first dark ditch you see. Anyway, you'd be doing me a favour to take it from me. It would help me in my purpose.'

Davie takes it. He puts it into the haversack and it drops down like a stone beside the sketch book and the coloured pencils and the fox mask and the antlers and the bara brith and Cheshire cheese.

'Thank you, lad,' says the priest. 'As each moment passes, I feel brighter, I feel lighter. The darkness slowly fades.'

He unfastens the buttons below his collar. He's wearing a blue T-shirt underneath. There is true bliss for a moment in his eyes.

'Ah, she is a smasher, Davie,' he whispers.

'That's good.'

'I thought it would be a fight, you know.'

'A fight?'

'Yes. I imagined that in order to free myself I would have to struggle and to fight with God. Perhaps that is because . . .'

He hesitates. He stares into the clear blue sky.

'Because what, Paddy?'

'Perhaps because, Davie, there is no God at all. Perhaps, Davie, because God is a figment of our own imaginations. Perhaps God is just a story that we like to tell ourselves.' His eyes widen in shock at his own words. 'What a thing for a priest to say!' he says. 'But the words have formed themselves and have left my lips and they have flown like birds into the air.'

He snatches at the air as if to catch the words that have left his lips. He opens his mouth wide and laughs as he pretends to throw the words back into it. 'No good,' he said. 'The words are spoke, the deed is done. Does it shock you, to hear a priest suggesting that there is no God at all?'

'No.'

'Of course it doesn't. You are a man of the modern world, Davie, and you are the first to know my news. I ask that you will keep it to yourself for now.'

'I will.'

'Good man. Thank you for passing by and for lending your ear to me. Doubtless there will be some trouble in my way, but then I think there will be much joy.'

'There will be.'

'Indeed there will. A few weeks back I would have asked you to pray for me, but now I ask you just to be yourself, to wander, to share this sunlit heaven with

Paddy Kelly and his love.'

'I will, Paddy.'

'And now I think that you are keen to wander on.' He winks. 'And look out for the murderers.'

'I will, Paddy.'

And Davie leaves, with the dreadful old prayer book in his sack, and wanders on uphill.

Of course, he wonders for a moment who Paddy Kelly's secret love might be, but there's no way to discover an answer to that. It is a mystery and must remain so for now, along with all the other mysteries of the world.

Walk on. Walk on.

Soon Davie is passing close to home. The entrance to his street is just off Felling Bank. He doesn't want to go there. The last thing he wants to do is to go home to tell Mam about a bloody murder so soon after the death of Dad. For a moment he has the image of the funeral cars coming slowly out of this entrance. He has the image of himself in a black car with a black tie around his neck. He has the image of the undertaker's driver dressed in black. Bleak, black memories. He doesn't want them. He turns away from them towards the light. As his mother said this morning, *The world is wide, the day is long, you're young and free.* And despite the dreadful event that's happened, the world is still wide, the day is still long, he is still young and free, and the last thing he wants is to go back home and for his mam to make him stay inside all day, to stay safe from the murderer.

So he keeps his head down and walks more quickly past that and past the entrance to his grandma and granddad's street and towards the hills and sky.

Then he slows down and breathes more easily and keeps on heading for the hills until he comes upon two little girls squatting on the ground at the junction with Balaclava Street, and one of them screams and says,

'Don't step on the fairies, you nit!'

SIX

He stops and steps back. They're drawing with chalk on the pavement. They've made a garden with trees and flowers and a blazing orange sun. One of the girls, who has bright ginger hair and is wearing a bright yellow dress, points down.

'There they are,' she says. 'See?'

'See what?'

'The fairies, silly,' says the other girl. She's wearing blue jeans and a white T-shirt and she has golden hair. 'And you nearly stepped on them, so that makes you a big daft nit!'

Davie crouches down beside them.

'Oh, yes,' he says.

Yes, two winged fairies dressed just like the girls but with wings at their backs, poised to take flight.

They've written a title across the top of the picture. *The Gardin of Fairys & Monstas.*

'Monsters?' he says.

'Yes,' says the red-haired girl. 'And don't you go thinking we can't spell, 'cos we can. It just looks better that way, doesn't it?'

He looks at the words. *Gardin. Fairys. Monstas.* The words do look better like that, written beautifully on the pavement. They're like something from a child's first writings, or like something from a dream, or like the lovely words you're not supposed to say.

'Yes,' he says. 'It does.'

'Of course it does. And there's a monster there, look.'

She points to a tall dark shape at the edge of a row of green trees.

'You can't make him out properly yet,' she says, ''cos he's hiding in the shadows and he hasn't got his proper shape yet. But he's going to cause big trouble if he gets his way. He's just waiting for his chance.'

'We draw the monsters with this,' says Goldenhair.

She points a thick stick at Davie. It's all burned and charred at the tip.

'We got this from the fire,' she says.

'Which fire?'

'The one on Balaclava Street. There's always a fire along there.'

'Where they burn the people they don't like!' giggles her friend.

Davie looks towards the entrance to Balaclava Street, a little further up the bank. He shivers.

'What's the monster called?' he asks.

'He's got no name. The horriblest monsters don't have names.'

'He's Mr Noname,' says the red-haired girl.

'Or The Nameless Horror,' says Goldenhair. 'What's your name? Mr Nit? Mr Dafty?'

'No. It's Davie.'

'Well, you could have been a monster with a name, couldn't you, if we hadn't stopped you? You could have put your big daft feet on our precious fairies and squashed them flat and you could have been Davie the Dreadful Monster!'

'I'm sorry,' Davie says. 'I didn't see. What are the fairies' names?'

'Catherine and Lara,' they say together.

'And what are your names?'

They giggle and squeak.

'Catherine and Lara!' they say together.

'I'm Catherine,' says the red-haired girl.

'So you must be Lara,' says Davie to Goldenhair.

'I must be!'

'The garden looks great,' he says.

And it does. Lovely shapes and colours on the pavement in the bright sunlight. A world created by two lasses with coloured chalks on the pathways of the town.

'We're going to make it bigger,' says Lara. 'We're starting here but we're going to fill all the pavements in the town with pictures and make a whole world of fairies and monsters and lots of other things.'

'What kind of other things?'

'Magic things, of course,' she says. 'Unicorns and elves and . . .'

'And lots more monsters,' says Catherine. 'And ogres and fiends hiding in holes.'

'And ghosts,' says Lara. 'And . . . snakes and wolves and wild cats.'

'And angels in the sky,' says Catherine.

'What about people?' Davie asks.

'Oh, there'll be people,' says Catherine. 'There'll be people, just like in the world.'

'And will they be happy?'

'Oh, yes,' says Lara. 'Just like we are. But they'll have to be careful.'

'Because of the monsters?' says Davie.

'Yes, because the monsters and snakes might get them!' says Catherine.

'And they've got to be good,' says Lara, 'or we'll just scribble them out!'

'And there'll be other kinds of people too,' says Lara. 'There'll be people with claws and people with wings and people with . . .'

'Horns!' says Catherine.

'Yes!' says Lara. 'And people with hooves instead of feet. And . . .'

'And people with feathers!' says Catherine. 'And people with scales! And . . .'

'That all sounds great,' says Davie.

'It is!' says Catherine. 'Our garden will be a world of wonders!'

They both squeak and giggle.

'We're just like little gods, aren't we?' says Catherine.

'You are,' says Davie.

'And if it ever rains and washes it all away,' says Lara, 'then we'll just have to start again and make it all again.'

'Yes,' says Catherine. 'It is our life's purpose.'

They giggle and squeak.

'It's brilliant!' says Davie.

'Thank you,' says Lara. 'I bet you couldn't do something like this.'

''Course he couldn't,' says Catherine. 'He's just a big daft nitty lad.'

Davie's about to get his pencils and sketch book out to show them, but he doesn't get a chance.

'Anyway,' says Lara, 'that's quite enough of that, thank you very much. We don't have time for lads like you. We have lots to get on with.'

He doesn't move.

'The garden and the creatures won't make themselves, you know!' says Catherine.

'So go on,' says Lara. 'Off you go.'

'OK.'

'And just watch where you're walking.'

'I will,' says Davie.

He steps around them and around their picture.

They giggle and squeak.

'Goodbye, Mr Nit,' they say together.

He walks away, careful where he steps, but he can't pass by Balaclava Street, the place of endless fire.

SEVEN

He was told many times when he was little not to come here.

This is Craig country.

'They're decent enough people when they're on their own,' his dad once said. 'And it even seems they might be related to us in some way . . .'

'Related to us?' said Davie.

'Aye. But then everybody's probably related to everybody in a little place like this, if you go back far enough. In fact, we're related to everybody in the world, if you go back far enough. And to every beast in the world, if you go even further. The point is, when they're together in their clan, that's when they can get nasty, even to bairns. So just keep away.'

Did Davie believe him? He probably did. Little kids

like to be told where the wild places are and who the wild people are. But he soon understood that his dad was exaggerating so he could keep his son safe. Davie knew some of the Craig kids at school and they were OK. Some of them even seemed nice, though you wouldn't want to make them your proper friends.

Anyway, he'd looked along the road many times when he was growing up. Had never entered it. No need to. There was nobody he wanted to see along there, and it leads to nowhere else, just circles a green at the far end and comes back out again. A cul-de-sac.

But today everything feels so different, and Davie's not that little kid any more. He stands at the junction and he looks. There are the grass verges with the tall plane trees growing. There's the cracked roadway. There's the long double row of terraced brick houses with short gardens and low fences in front. Smoke is rising from the chimneys, even on a day like today. There's smoke rising from the green as well, where the endless fire must be. And there's a tall pole, with what looks like some kind of head on top.

He steps forward. He feels his heart thumping. *Don't be stupid*, he tells himself. *Don't be scared. It's just a street. It's just another place in your own home town. The people are people, just like yourself. And you're only a quarter of a mile or so from your own front door.* And it all seems very peaceful. The news mustn't have come this far yet.

There's kids playing in the gardens and on the distant green. A few dogs are roaming. Woman stand together, gossiping. Blokes hunch low, smoking and muttering to each other.

Davie keeps going, slowly.

On the fence is scrawled in black paint:

CRAIGS 4 EVER

There's a skull and crossbones.

KILL ALL KILLENS

He keeps on going. A couple of dogs watch him, but no one pays him much attention. *They're not bothered*, he tells himself. *You can turn around at any time and come back out.* He gets closer to the green. He can hardly breathe. *Don't be stupid*, he tells himself again. *Just calm down.* He's just about to turn around.

Then they get him.

They're smaller and younger than him but there are four of them and they know how to grab somebody and to keep them grabbed and how to make them hurt. They've got stripes of paint on their faces. One of them's wearing an ancient-looking feathered head dress. Another's wearing a necklace of what look like teeth. He's got a tomahawk shoved into the top of his jeans.

'Who are ye?' one of them asks.

'Where you come from?'

'What's yer name?'

'Are you a Killen?'

He says nothing. They drag and shove him towards the green. They're laughing like monsters and giggling like the little girls. A couple of blokes are watching. They're shaking their heads and grinning.

'Leave the poor lad alone!' comes a woman's voice.

They keep on dragging him.

He sees that there is some kind of animal skull at the top of the pole. They see him looking.

'That's how the last kid that wandered in here ended up!' one says.

Davie knows that isn't true. It's the head of a dog or a deer, some poor creature. There are scratched words and drawings on the pole and painted curses. There are scrawled drawings of devils and ghouls. The smoke from the fire drifts around it. The fire is small, just a low smouldering thing at the middle of a big ring of black ash and cinders. The whole place smells of smoke and ash. The whole place feels as hot as hell.

'I said, leave the lad alone!' comes the voice again.

The kids take no notice. A couple of dogs are here now. They keep yelping, snarling.

'Tie him up!' says one of the kids.

They scream with laughter at the idea. Davie tries to resist. He tries to dig in his heels but it's no good. They get him to the pole. A bigger boy comes. He's naked to the waist, and has a long thin rope in his hands. There's a tattoo of a wolf on his chest.

He laughs softly, even gently.

'What you doing here, you daft bugger?' he says to Davie.

Davie knows him. He's seen him at school. He's a couple of years older. He's seen him wandering around town in Wranglers and a Ben Sherman. He's seen him underneath a cherry tree with a girl in Holly Hill Park.

He pulls Davie's haversack off. Then he grabs Davie's hands and yanks them backwards and ties them together behind the pole. The rope digs into Davie's skin and it stings.

Then they all stand in front of him and laugh at what they've done.

'What's yer name?' says the older boy.

There's stubble on his lip and chin.

'I said, what's yer name?'

Davie tells him.

'Good lad, Davie,' he says. 'My name is Fernando.'

Everyone giggles.

Fernando keeps on laughing softly.

'Forgive them,' he says. 'They're a bit overexcited today.'

'Leave the lad alone!' comes the voice again.

Fernando opens the haversack.

'What have we got here? Ah, Davie has brought a pie for us.'

He munches into it, then passes it to the others.

'Now be nice,' he tells them, 'and share and share alike.'

He smiles broadly as they eat. He tries to give the last tiny piece to Davie but Davie just spits it out.

Fernando shakes his head in disappointment.

'One of the children could have had that,' he says.

He opens the haversack again.

'Oh, look, children,' he says. 'Coloured pencils and a book. How very nice! Shall we make some pretty pictures?'

'Leave him *alone!*'

One of the kids runs off to a house. He comes back with a handful of tomatoes.

'Me mam says we can fling these at him,' he says. 'They're turning rotten.'

So they stand in front of Davie and throw them. He gets splattered.

Fernando's looking through the book. He's scribbling with some of the pencils.

'Get off them!' Davie says.

'Or what?' laughs Fernando.

He starts writing or drawing in it. He keeps on looking at Davie and at the pole and the fire. He seems almost kind when his eyes meet Davie's.

'Keep still, will ye?' he says. 'Stop lolloping about. I'm trying to get you right!' He laughs. 'I'm trying to make you handsome.'

Davie stares back at him. Could they be related? Is Fernando's face a bit like his own? Is that how Davie will look in a couple of years' time?

Another kid comes with an armful of sticks and logs and an old broken chair. He throws them on to the fire and they blaze to life.

'Let's burn him!' he says.

'Aye! That'll learn him!'

'Get him in the fire!' they chant. 'In the fire! In the fire!'

Davie starts to shudder. He can't help himself. He's going to cry.

'In the fire! Chop his head off! Put his skull on top!'

They start to stamp the earth. They yell at the skull on top of the pole.

'Great God of the Pole!' they yell. 'Look down upon us as we prepare this sacrifice!'

They dance and swirl.

'We offer this creature up to you!' they yell.

They howl and laugh.

Fernando calmly keeps on drawing. He holds the book up to compare the lad in there with the lad that's tied to the pole. He makes more marks.

He regards what he has done.

'Yes,' he says. 'Very good, though I say it myself.'

He winks.

'And, yes,' he says. 'I have made you handsome, Davie.'

The fire crackles. Smoke swirls around Davie. Sparks sting his cheeks.

The kids howl, dance and laugh.

'The time of Death is almost upon us!' they yell.

A couple of blokes start walking slowly towards the pole. One of them puts his hand up.

'Now then, lads . . .' he starts.

Everybody pauses. There's a police car coming along the road. It parks at the edge of the green.

Two policemen get out of it. The silver on their helmets glints in the sunlight. They amble across the grass.

'What is gannin on here?' says the tallest one.

'We're just playing, officer,' says one of the kids.

'Doesn't look like playing to me. Set him loose.'

Fernando winks and puts the pencils and book back into the haversack and hands it over. He starts to untie Davie. He does it gently. He kisses Davie quickly on the cheek.

'Nice to meet you, Davie,' he whispers.

Davie recoils. His wrists are stinging. He scrapes the tomatoes off.

'What's your name, son?' says the shorter policeman.

'Davie,' says Davie.

'And what might have caused you to come along here, Davie?'

'I don't know.'

'You don't *know*. Are you mental?'

'I don't think so.'

'Are you injured?'

The little boy in Davie wants to sob and to tell him about his wrists and his cheeks and the tomatoes.

But he just says, no, he's not.

'That's good. Now listen. We've got bigger fish to fry today, so mebbe you should just get yourself away while you can. OK?'

'OK,' says Davie.

'And you won't be daft enough to come back here again, will you, Davie?'

'No,' he says.

'Good lad,' says his partner.

Then he turns to the watching Craigs.

'Now then,' he says. 'Have any of you lot seen Zorro today?'

Davie puts his haversack on and can't stop himself from starting to run.

He pauses beside the girls at the entrance.

'Did you have a nice time?' says Lara.

She points the burned stick at him.

She pokes his chest and leaves a black ashy mark there.

'Fancy going in there!' she says. 'What a daft nit!'

He's about to hurry on, then he sees the Killens, gathering on the pavements and verges.

EIGHT

They have dogs. They're carrying sticks. There are a dozen or more of them, squatting on the verges, leaning against gate posts and garden walls. There are kids as young as Catherine and Lara, teenagers like him, and older ones. Davie's instinct is just to hurry home, to get back to his house, to his mother, to the smell of lemon meringue and bara brith. But whichever way he goes he has to pass by them, to pass through them. A girl comes to him. He's seen her around. She knows him too. She's about his age. He's seen her laughing and smiling. He's seen her with boys in the park, boys he knows, boys he'd like to be like. Today her eyes are cold. Her hands are tightened into fists.

'What you doing in there?' she says.

'What?' he stammers.

'What you doing in there? You're not a Craig, are you?'

'N-no.'

'Are you on their side?'

The question is stupid. He knows that, but he can't say that.

'No.'

'Do you know what they've done?'

'Yes.'

A man comes. He has long black hair, thick sideburns, broad shoulders, strong arms.

'You were down there, weren't you?' he says. 'At the church hall?'

'Yes.'

'You saw dead Jimmy, didn't you?'

'Y-yes.'

'Let him go,' he says to the girl. 'Nobody should have to see that, 'specially a kid like this one is.'

'What do you mean, like this one is?' she says.

'He's not been brung up to face up to it, not like we have.'

He reaches out and rests his hand on Davie's shoulder for a moment.

'You believe in peace, don't you?' he says. 'You

believe everybody should get along, don't you?'

'Yes,' says Davie.

'Good lad. We need good lads like you in this dark and troubled world.'

Beyond the man, other Killens are arriving, singly and in little groups.

The man tilts his head to the side.

'Your dad believed in that as well,' he says.

Davie catches his breath.

'You *knew* him?' he says.

'Went to school with him, long ago.'

He smiles.

'You look surprised, son. It's a little town, isn't it? 'Course we went to school together. Played football on the fields together.'

He smiles again.

'We were almost pals, till the day he saw me thrashing Sebastian Craig in the school yard one day. Then he kept his distance. And who could blame him?'

Davie looks at the man. He doesn't know what to say to that.

'Me name's Anthony Killen,' says the man. He puts out his hand and Davie takes it. 'I hope you're right and we will all live in peace one day. But in the meantime there's much battling to do.'

He steps aside as if to let Davie pass.

'I kept on seeing him through the years. He was a good soul. He was kind to me when we lost our little Alice. I poured my heart out to him, if the truth be told.'

His eyes glaze over for a moment.

'I'm sorry for your loss, son,' he says.

Then he turns to the girl.

'Let him go,' he says. 'Let him pass.'

The girl steps away. Others step aside. Davie walks.

Behind him a low chanting starts.

Killens kill

Killens kill

Killens kill

Killens kill!

Feet start stamping on the pavement. Dogs start barking, howling.

Once he's free, Davie turns and sees the policemen standing at the entrance to Balaclava Street, close to where Catherine and Lara are. The girls go on with their work, as if oblivious to what's happening around them.

Davie walks. He thinks of Peace. He thinks of Death.

NINE

More Killens are coming downhill as he is going up.

There's a bunch of children with war paint on their faces and sticks carved into the shapes of swords in their hands.

'Which side are ye on?' yells a little girl in blonde pigtails and with black and orange stripes on her face. 'The Killens' or the Craigs'?'

She runs closer when he doesn't answer.

She giggles as she raises her wooden sword.

She can't be more than six or seven.

'Whose side?' she says again.

'Go away,' he tells her. 'Don't be so stupid.'

She giggles again.

'I can't,' she says. 'We're gannin to war!'

Her friends call her back to them.

She leaves him and joins them.

They bounce their open palms against their mouths and make whooping howling noises, the kind that the Indians make in *The Lone Ranger*. They stamp their feet and dance and for minutes they get lost in the wildness of it, swirling and howling together, dancing in circles together beneath the blazing sun.

He walks on.

His breathing and heart start to slow as he gets closer to the allotments on Windy Ridge. He drops down on to a wide verge under an ash tree. Yes, he cries a little as he leans against the trunk and brushes the tomato seeds and flesh off himself, as he rubs his wrists and rubs his cheeks with spit. *What a mess I must look*, he thinks. He opens the book to see Fernando's drawing of himself. He sighs to see how beautiful it is, how beautifully drawn and shaded, even though the boy at the heart of it is wide-mouthed and wide-eyed in terror, even though Fernando has drawn the cry coming from the boy's mouth, a cry that winds up around the pole and around the skull on top and all the way up into the wide blue sky.

AAAAAAAAAAGGGGGGGGHHHHHHHHH!!!!

Davie stays here for a while. The book rests in his lap.

He thinks about Fernando Craig. Like his dad said, if you go back far enough, everyone must be related to everyone. We're all from different strands of a single ancient family. But could Fernando be really close, some kind of second or third cousin or something? Is he really like Davie? He thinks about Fernando's chest and his wolf tattoo and his weirdly kind eyes and his voice and the way the little kids responded to him and the way the lass in Holly Hill Park was holding him. He thinks of Fernando's quick kiss on his cheek. And he thinks of how beautifully he draws. And Davie knows that part of him would love to be like Fernando. And he could have been just like him, if he'd been born a Craig, if he'd grown up on Balaclava Street. And when he thinks about that he knows that Zorro Craig could have been just like him. And Davie knows he could have been any of those Killens that he walked through as they prepared for war. He could have been Jimmy Killen. It could have been Davie lying there on the rubble of the church hall, dead.

He turns the page and draws a part of *The Gardin of Fairys and Monstas*, and, like Lara and Catherine, he dreams of the garden creeping inch by inch through the whole town. He dreams of angels flying high above.

He dreams of creatures that are half-human, half-beast, prowling through the town.

It calms him down. He keeps on drawing. He loses himself in drawing, wondering, dreaming. He ponders the idea that God, if he did exist, could be a kind of artist, creating worlds on pavements or pages with coloured pencils or chalk. He looks towards the emptiness above. He tries to imagine a god far beyond the wide blue sky, sitting beneath a tree with a book spread on his lap and with coloured pencils in his hands. He grins.

'Hello, God,' he whispers.

He wonders further. Maybe God is a kind of writer, endlessly composing stories. Maybe Davie's just part of one of those stories. Maybe he's just black words on a white page. But how could he be? He looks at his hands and arms, at his legs stretched out on the grass. They can't be just words, can they? He's troubled by the thought, and by the thought that if the story is already written then he has no choice in what he does or where he goes. Then he just laughs. He looks into the empty spaces around him like he's looking out from a page into the eyes of someone looking down at him.

'Hello, Reader,' he whispers. 'My name is Davie. Who are you?'

No answer, of course.

He says it again.

'Hello, Reader. Who are you?'

Then there's a padding, a snuffling. Hell's teeth. It's the slobbery dog from outside the Columba Club. It pads towards Davie with its tongue dangling from its wet gob.

'What you doing here?' says Davie.

It says nothing, of course.

'Go away,' he tells it.

He waves his hands at it.

He pretends to be about to throw a rock at it.

'Get lost!' he says.

But it just stands and watches Davie like it wants something or like it's just dead stupid.

Davie draws a quick picture of it with black and brown pencils and makes it really ugly, then he scribbles all over it so it's nothing but a meaningless scrawl. He shows the page to the dog.

'Look,' he says. 'I've made you and got rid of you. You're dead, like Stew. So disappear.'

It doesn't disappear.

Davie stands up and tries to look as if he's going to kick it.

That just makes it mad.

It bares its teeth and snarls.

Stupid dog.

It does move away but it turns back to stare at him, as if it wants him to follow. Davie gives up. He puts his stuff away and lifts the haversack to his back and follows. He was going that way, anyway. He walks on the narrow pathway by the allotments. He tries to take no notice of the dog, but he can't not see it just a few paces ahead, can't not hear it, panting and slobbering.

So horrible.

TEN

'What's its name?'

Davie stops suddenly and blinks.

There's a bloke leaning on his allotment fence. He's grinning.

'You're in a dream, son, aren't you? I said, what's his name?'

'Whose name?'

'Your dog's.'

'He isn't mine.'

'Ah. Just taken to you, has he?'

'Aye.'

'That's the way of them, the devils.'

He reaches over as if he wants to stroke the dog but it backs away. The bloke laughs.

'You don't know me, do you?' he says.

Now he mentions it, he does look kind of familiar to Davie.

'I knew your dad,' says the bloke.

Oh, aye, thinks Davie. *I've seen him around. He was at the funeral.*

'Used to have a pint with him in the Columba,' says the bloke. 'He was a good man. But you know that, don't you?'

'Aye.'

There's a smell of opened earth and growing vegetables and creosote from the fence. There are hens clucking, and bees drone as they drift from bloom to bloom. The greenhouses glitter and sparkle in the sunlight. The sun is high above the crest of the hill, pouring and pouring its light and heat down upon everything.

'I'm Oliver Henderson,' says the bloke.

He reaches over the fence and Davie shakes his hand.

He has loose green overalls on and he's as brown as a nut. His green eyes glint as he looks and speaks. He reaches into a pocket and holds out a pear.

'You'll need the juice as much as anything,' he says. 'Summers like this just dry you out. You found that?'

Davie bites into the pear and shrugs.

'You won't have. Not yet. Too young. The last summer I knew like this was when my Angela was still with us.'

The pear is delicious. Davie catches its juices with his tongue. He feels its sweetness spreading through him.

They hear the calling of larks from high above, of children from far away. In some nearby street, a motorbike sputters and roars and moves away and disappears into the northern distance, and the children and the larks remain. A siren starts up in the town below, wails for a few moments then falters and stops.

'I'm finding it's a good year for peas,' says Oliver. 'And the brassicas are doing well, as long as I keep on top of the watering, and as long as the damn deer keep away.'

'The deer?' says Davie.

'Aye. They've been coming down from over the top. And they love them blimmin' cabbages.'

He has an accent from further north, from Northumberland. Softer vowels than Davie's. The 'R's are sounded in the back of his throat and his voice rolls over them. Davie listens. The sounds are so rich, so tender.

'Surprising, isn't it?' he says. 'Wild deer coming down into our little town. Lovely beggars they are too, despite the havoc they bring. They're beasts to be welcomed. Beautiful things. Sometimes at dusk I've seen them coming down, a little family of them.'

Oliver turns and points across the allotments towards the fields above. Davie sees children running where he points and beyond them a great red drift of poppies.

'They come over from the wild side and down through them poppies. See them?' Oliver says. 'Second flush this year. Best flush any year.'

The poppies glow bright red against the green. They shimmer in the light.

'Dusk's the best,' he says. 'When the sky begins to burn and the poppies start to glow and the shadows of the deer prowl and wild black starlings swirl in massive clouds above.'

He smiles.

'Sometimes I think I'm turning to an old fool,' he says. 'I'm losing me mind to the beauty of the world and one day I'll be lost in it for ever. I'll be standing here at the fence, but the real me will be gone, lost in the starlings and the deer and the poppies and the setting sun . . .'

He grins as his voice peters out.

'Tek no notice, lad,' he says. 'But you passing by with the dog gives us a chance to blather on. Heading upward, eh?'

'Aye.'

'A good direction to go.'

'You've not seen Zorro Craig, have you?'

'Zorro Craig? I don't know the feller, so I wouldn't know if I had. What's he look like?'

'Just a lad. Dark hair. He'd've been running, if it was him.'

'No. Sorry. Mind you, I do get lost in the contemplation of me brassicas and peas.'

Oliver doesn't mention the death, the murder. Maybe he knows nothing about it yet. Maybe the news hasn't travelled so high yet. Davie doesn't tell him, doesn't want to disturb the peace.

'I did see a running lass, though,' says Oliver.

'A running lass?'

'Aye, dressed all in blue with her black hair flying, dashing up the allotment path.'

He closes his eyes.

'Bonny, she was,' he says. 'Running like she had a wind behind her and wings at her back.'

He smiles. He reaches into another pocket.

'And I get lost in the contemplation of these sweet little beggars too.'

He takes out a tiny bright yellow chick. He cups it in his hand. So soft, so bright, so trembling, so alive.

'Come into the world just two short days ago. You want to hold her?'

Davie puts his hand out. He takes the chick into his cupped palm. There's hardly any weight to it at all. He raises it to his eyes and gazes at it. How can anything be so yellow? How can anything be so frail and yet so filled with life? How can anything take such a shape? How can anything be anything?

'Three days back,' says Oliver, 'she was a lump of feathery gloop squashed into a shell. Weeks before that she was nothing at all. And now she's come out and she's the colour of the sun that's shining down on her. How can something like that come about?'

He looks at Davie as if he expects an answer.

Davie shakes his head.

'Nobody really knows, Mr Henderson,' he says.

'Aye, that's right. Nobody knows, it's all a mystery

and it keeps on happening and happening and happening. And I wake up every day this summer and I come into this garden, and every day I'm . . .' He stares at the sky, seeking a word. '. . . I'm astonished, I'm astounded, I'm absolutely flabbergasted, lad.'

Davie passes back the chick. Oliver takes it, puts it into his pocket again.

'Of course, the thing to protect him from is Mr Fox, who's another wild and wanton visitor to these parts at night. You ever hear him calling?'

Davie thinks of his own fox cries. He doesn't even know how close they are to true fox cries or whether they just pour out of him.

'I don't think so,' he says.

'You will, if you listen hard enough and deep enough on a still and silent night. It's a screech to chill your blood.'

Davie ponders that. It will be something to listen for, something to remember.

'So has he got something you're wanting?' says Oliver.

'Who?' Davie says.

'This Zorro lad.'

'Oh. I'm not sure, really.' Davie laughs. 'I'm not

sure I even want to find him, really.'

Oliver laughs too, and gives Davie another pear. He tells him to keep it for the journey. Davie puts it into the sack.

'Thank you,' he says.

Oliver contemplates the boy.

'You think I'm kind, don't you?' he says.

'Yes. I think so.'

'I am, Davie. I'm known for it. And these hands are tender.'

He holds them out, his hands. Davie sees the intricate patterns on them, the dark garden dirt caught in the creases.

'They turn the earth,' says Oliver. 'They plant seeds and they pick fruit and vegetables and flowers. They tend newborn chicks.'

Davie wants to reach and touch them, to run his fingertips across the skin of this man.

Oliver knows that.

'Go on, son,' he says. 'Touch them.'

So Davie does that. The skin is rough and dry. He can feel the muscles and bones beneath. Oliver turns his hands over and Davie touches the smoother skin there, feels the strong tendons, touches the knuckles, the nails. He used to touch his dad's hands in the same way, back when he was young. It was an intense and simple joy, to touch the man who was his father. He remembers how they laughed together when Davie ran his finger across his dad's palm to tickle him. And how tender his dad's hands felt when they tousled his hair or stroked his cheek. And how strong and safe they felt when they gripped him and raised him high into the air and when his dad called out from below,

'Go on, my Davie! Fly!'

Oliver smiles gently. He touches Davie's cheek.

'Good lad,' he whispers, just like Davie's dad used to.

'But,' says Oliver, closing his hands and letting them hang at his side, 'these hands have been with me to war, Davie. And I should tell you that I strangled three men with them on a summer's night.'

He tilts his head to the side and regards the boy.

'I'm a killer,' he says. 'A strangler.'

He pauses, allowing Davie to ponder this new fact.

'You ever known a killer before?' he says.

Davie shakes his head, and remembers a morning a few years back. His dad had bought him a toy gun for his birthday. It was a plastic thing, just like the shotgun they used on stagecoaches in *The Lone Ranger* to kill pursuing bandits and renegade Indians. His dad grinned with pleasure as he demonstrated how to put the gun to the shoulder, how to peer through the sights, how to squeeze the trigger and fire imaginary bullets at some unsuspecting passer-by.

'You're dead,' said Dad.

They both laughed.

'Everybody likes to get a gun in their hand, eh?' said Dad.

He fired again.

'You're dead!' he said again.

Then held the gun, admired it, passed it back to his son.

'Your turn,' he said, and Davie started squeezing the trigger and firing bullets and sending imaginary people to their imaginary deaths.

A siren sounds again, calls Davie out of the memory, and it seems so far away, as if it's in another world.

'My dad went to war,' he says to Oliver.

'I know that, son. And he was a tender man like me, wasn't he?'

'Yes.'

Yes. Of course his dad was tender. But he knew

nothing about his time at war.

'Would my dad do what you did?' Davie asks.

'Who knows?' says Oliver. 'Maybe he would, if he had to. But if he had, I suppose he wouldn't tell his own son about it when the son was still a bairn.'

Davie tugs at the haversack straps. He feels its weight on his back. When Dad took it out of a high cupboard and passed it on, he said,

'This sack's been all the way to war and back, Davie.'

Davie hears his voice in his ear, his breath on his cheek.

'Now carry it through the peace,' Dad whispered.

Oliver's smiling gently.

'You keep slipping into a dream, don't you?' he says.

Davie shrugs and smiles.

'Into dreams and memories,' he says.

'That's all right,' says Oliver. 'Sometimes a memory or a dream is a fine place to be. And sometimes it can seem like everything is just a dream. Don't you think that?'

'Yes,' says Davie. 'I do.'

They're silent for a moment.

'It had to be done,' says Oliver. 'It had to be done in silence on that summer's night those years ago. It was the only thing to do. I was the only one to do it.'

He sighs.

'It's all a mystery,' he says. 'Isn't it? Poppies and starlings, newborn chicks as bright as the sun, ugly dogs, gardeners' hands that care and kill.'

He watches Davie.

'It is, isn't it?' he repeats.

'Aye. It's all a mystery, Mr Henderson.'

'They should just have chosen two, shouldn't they?'

Davie doesn't know what he's on about.

'Two men,' says Oliver. 'They should have chosen a man from either side and let them fight it out. No need for all that war. No need for bullets and bombs. No need for all that slaughter. No need for three lads to be strangled. No need for men like me to turn to stranglers. Just two men fighting to the death and letting that be a start and end to it.'

'Aye,' says Davie. 'It would have been better.'

But he remembers the delight of the kids in Balaclava Street as they hauled him to the fire. He remembers the determination of the gathering Killen clan. He remembers his dad's contentment when he held the toy gun in his hands.

'Good lad,' says Oliver Henderson. 'Walk on in

peace. I hope you find your Zorro Craig. You'll say hello on your way back down again?'

'I will.'

And on goes Davie, with the ugly dog in front.

ELEVEN

Two ladies in a garden before a house on Windy Ridge.

'You're Davie, aren't you?' says one of them in a low voice as he passes by.

She's Letitia Spall. He knows her. The one beside her is unknown. They both have arms folded beneath their breasts. There are dazzling hip-high flowers, perhaps dahlias, glowing all around them.

'I see your mother's face in you,' says Letitia. 'I see your father's too.'

Davie wants to move on but the words cause him to hesitate.

'I knew you when you were a babe,' she continues. 'I remember I slipped a coin one day into the covers on your pram. You were a bonny bairn. I see that bonny bairn in you as well.'

She smiles and leans closer.

Her companion smiles as well.

'I didn't know you when you were a bairn,' she says. 'But that's not too surprising. I come from Hexham, from far beyond the far side of the hill, and didn't know these parts at all until I came to know Letitia, and began to come across the hill to spend my time with her. My name is Annie, Davie. I am pleased to meet you, son.'

The ladies lean towards each other, their shoulders touch.

Behind and above them, a bedroom window of the house is wide open, a white net curtain drifts before it in the gentle breeze.

An orange butterfly lands on Letitia's shoulder. She whispers to it that it is welcome there.

Davie smiles, moves to move on.

'We were talking of the buzzards,' says Letitia.

'Of the buzzards?' says Davie.

'Aye,' says Letitia. 'And of the vulnerability of all babes.'

'Look high,' says Annie. 'And peel your eyes.'

They all turn their faces to the summit and to the light beyond. There are larks there, Davie knows, that are invisible.

'They are there, the buzzards,' she says, 'if you're able to look hard enough.'

So Davie looks as hard as he is able, and turns his eyes and mind from the two ladies, from gardens and allotments and from playing fields and drifts of poppies, and from the hill above him which he will climb, and, yes, at last he sees them, two dark birds with wings outstretched, wheeling in the blue. Two tiny birds, which must be massive to be seen from here so far below. Two massive birds above the place to which he seems to be heading as he wanders through the day.

'We talked,' says Letitia, 'of a tale that was told to me so long ago when I was little more than a babe myself.'

Davie turns his eyes from the distant birds to the nearby lady.

'I was told,' she continues, 'that one summer morning, bright and warm as this one is, a buzzard dropped from its distant sky to the air above these gardens. It dropped down to a basket on a table in which a little babe was fast asleep, and that it took that babe in its claws and carried it away.'

'And I said,' says her companion, Annie, 'that such a thing would be impossible. A little babe, no matter how tiny it might have been, would be an impossible thing for a bird such as a buzzard to lift. What do you think, bonny lad?'

'I suppose,' says Davie, 'that I think it'd be impossible as well.'

'And yet,' says Letitia, 'I was told that such a thing indeed was true. And in my bairn-ness, I believed it. And I was told that the mother and the father and the brother of the babe rushed out of this house and from this gate, and hurried upward across the fields, all the time calling to the bird above to give them back the little bairn they loved so much. But the bird continued upward, and the tiny babe continued dangling from its claws.'

She pauses, to allow Davie to look once more towards the sky above the hill, to imagine there the upward-flapping bird, the dangling babe. *Would the babe*, he wonders, *have been screaming? Would it understand that now it was exposed in air, when once it was at home on earth? Would it perhaps accept that this was just the fate of all babes born on to this earth?*

And he imagines the frantic family beneath. He imagines them howling at the sky, holding out their arms in case the babe should fall.

'A bird,' goes on Letitia, 'can fly through air much quicker than a man, a woman or a boy can run across the earth. Soon, because of shrubs and trees and rocks, they could not always keep the bird in sight.'

'Can you imagine it?' says Annie. 'I'm sure that I cannot. Perhaps a buzzard could carry a babe as far as a garden gate, perhaps even as far as an allotment row, but surely it couldn't carry a babe as far as that! Couldn't carry it, as Letitia told me, until it hovered a hundred feet over the summit of the hill with the babe in its sharp claws, while the desperate family sprinted, gasped, grunted in useless hot pursuit.'

'But that's the tale that was told to me,' Letitia continues, 'the tale that has lodged itself deep in my heart, so that at my age now, I hardly care if it's true or not. I care only for the strangeness and the beauty and the terror of it. The bird went out of sight, Davie. The sky was empty but for the everlasting larks. And the family reached the summit and they wept to know such loss. And then they roamed the high land, until the boy, the brother, began to call, "There! There! Hear it? Hear it?" And he led the mother and the father towards what he had heard, the weeping of a baby.'

'They found it?' says Davie.

'They hurried to the sound. And, oh, they found a baby lying on green turf beside a trickling stream.'

'*A* baby?' says Davie. 'It wasn't theirs?'

'Ah, at first they said they couldn't be certain.'

'Couldn't be *certain*?'

'They said at first they thought the baby's crying voice had changed its tone. They thought the eyes were a brighter blue than they'd been before. And when they came to it, it did not stretch its arms out to them as it would have done before. But then they calmed, they knew that it must be their own babe.'

'Who else's could it be?'

'No one else's, of course. They said afterwards that their perception of the babe had been confounded by their terror. They said that it wouldn't be surprising if a babe did not undergo some changes after the experience of such an ambushment, and such a flight into the sky. They lifted the babe, they carried it home to Windy Ridge, where it was loved, they said, as no other babe has ever been loved, and it grew and flourished as all babes seem to do in this place.'

She reaches out and tousles Davie's hair.

'As you do yourself, Davie, despite all toils and torments.' She narrows her eyes as she peers at him.

'Oh, I remember you, the bonny babe beneath the covers in the pram with everything before him. And I see you now, all grown up and walking in the gorgeous light with everything before him still. I see the babe, the boy, the man you will become. I see the changes that have happened and the changes still to come. Your mother must be proud of you. Oh, how you have changed.'

Her companion laughs.

'Of course he's changed,' she says. 'But it didn't take an ambushment by a buzzard on a summer day to bring the change about.' She bites her lip and stares into Davie's eyes. 'Or *did* it?' she says. 'Have you been lifted from the earth in terror, lad?'

Davie laughs out loud at the thought.

'I don't think so,' he says. 'I don't remember it!'

They watch him and wait.

'And my journey to the summit of the hill,' he says, 'is much slower than the baby's or its family was.'

'It was the babe herself who told the tale to me,' says Letitia.

'The babe?'

'The babe who by then had grown into a woman old enough to have babies of her own. She had been told that this had happened to her many years ago, before she could remember anything.'

'And she believed it?'

'She said that she believed it. Ha. And she said that sometimes she believed that she was not the babe they had pursued, but was a babe from somewhere far across the hill, laid down there by that buzzard or another buzzard. She said that maybe she was the wrong baby. She talked of going on a journey some time, to find out if there was another baby dropped down by a buzzard. She wondered if the real she was someone else to be discovered somewhere else.'

She touches the orange butterfly. It flaps and floats away from her shoulder.

'Anyway,' says Letitia Spall, 'what are such tales but beautiful distractions on such a perfect day as this?'

At the bedroom window, the white net curtains drift. The ladies lean together, smiling.

Annie winks.

'Perhaps,' she says, 'the tale she tells is the tale of Letitia Spall herself.'

The ladies laugh.

'Tell your mam that I was asking,' says Letitia. 'My sympathies to her and to you for your sad loss.'

She reaches out and tousles him again.

'Like the babe,' she says, 'what is lost might be discovered again, but in a different form, and the form might simply be a tale that could be lies and could be truths and could be lovely bits of both.'

She pushes a coin into his hand.

'Take this,' she says. 'It's like the coin I slipped between the covers in your pram when you were a tiny babe. It's for the future, as I whispered to sleeping tiny you, before you knew there was such a thing as future at all.'

Davie thanks her, and sighs, and turns away from the happy pair.

'Don't let the buzzards take you!' says Letitia Spall.

He laughs. He wanders on. He imagines the buzzard's claws on his shoulders. He imagines dark wings beating above his head. He imagines himself being lifted, his walking feet rising from the earth. He feels the warm breeze at his back.

TWELVE

He steps from the narrow allotment path on to the green grass of the fields. Everything's at peace, the way it was just yesterday. Loads of lads scuttle and swarm across the green in the distance, caught up in the everlasting football game. Mams push toddlers on swings in the little play park nearby. There's the rhythmical *squeak squeak squeak* of the swings and the giggles and the laughter and the high-pitched yells of, 'Higher, higher, higher, higher!' There's the grinding up and down of the ancient seesaw that's been there since Davie's mam was young. Lads and lasses stroll hand in hand or arm in arm. Others'll be further up the field, lying hidden in the long grass. And the larks sing high in the sky as they always do, no matter what dreadful things might have occurred on the earth below.

Davie walks. He's been this way a thousand times, but every time it seems so different and so strange, like he comes upon it every time so new. Or maybe it's because he's new every time, like every time he walks he's a different Davie to the one who walked before.

Heat and the scent of the dry earth rise from the grass. The air is all ashimmer. He hears the calling of his name from far away.

'Davie! Davie! Davie!'

Must be one of the footballers. He pauses and watches. They're swarming closer now. There are goals, but they've left these far behind. Two goalkeepers, tiny dark distant figures, guard them. It's one of the formless games. All ideas of a proper rectangular pitch are gone. A little leading bunch kick and dribble, trip and nudge. They blast the ball forward and hurry after it. Others swarm and follow. Some of the slower ones or younger ones have already given up. They're lounging on the grass, waiting, knowing that the game will return.

Davie hears his name again.

'Davie!'

It's a boy he's known since he was a toddler. Raymond Brooks. He's naked to the waist, as half the lads always are when they play on days like this. He runs out of the pack at Davie.

'Come and play, Davie! Skin or Top?'

'I can't,' says Davie. 'I've got no time.'

'You've got all the time in the world, man. It's the middle of the holidays. Skin or Top?'

Skin or Top? Does Davie want to join the half-naked team or the team that still has tops on?

'Be a Skin,' says Raymond. 'We need you. We're losing seven-two. Or eight-three.'

Davie thinks of the haversack. He can't take it off and leave it lying and run away from it.

'It'll have to be Tops,' he says.

He tightens the haversack straps.

Raymond's disappointed but he laughs.

'Davie's playing!' he yells. 'He's a Top.'

Somebody curls the ball towards Davie. He traps it but straight away he's tackled and it's gone. He runs, with the haversack bobbing and thumping at his back. He's in the crowd, three dozen or more boys and a couple of girls from across the town. They're kids of all ages, from five to seventeen. So many of them that hardly anybody gets a kick, and when the ball does come to you, all you can do is kick it on before somebody's barging into you or tripping you up. The stupid dog runs too, grunting and gasping and slobbering, twisting its way through the game. Davie yells at it to go away but of course it takes no notice. It yelps back at him, leaps at him. He runs away from it and it runs after him. The best players, Ronnie Hodgson or Leonard Hall, keep the ball for a short dribble, they swerve elegantly past a boy or two, but even they are quickly shoved aside, knocked over, dispossessed. Everybody's gasping, laughing, grunting, cursing. Everybody's lost in it. They all swarm back to where the game came from, towards the distant goals. Davie gets a kick or two. Once he manages to pass it accurately to another Top.

'Great ball, Davie!' comes the shout.

The blood is thumping through Davie's heart. His head is reeling with the effort and the heat. He runs. At times he stops to gasp and recover himself just like all the others do and then runs on again. They're a frantic crowd, in love with each other and the game. At moments they're famous players in a famous stadium, then they're what they really are – kids from Tyneside in jeans and battered trainers on a field with all of Tyneside down below, with the river snaking to the dark distant sea.

He gets the ball again. He drops his shoulder, feints, beats another player and kicks it on. Back they go towards the goals. The goalkeepers are ready now. They tug at their gloves, swing their arms, bob from side to side between their posts. The players are all back inside the rectangle where the faded pitch lines are. Every one of them yearns to be the one to score. Each player dreams of rising to head home a cross, of curving the ball so sweetly into the top corner, of chipping the ball over the spread-eagled keeper, of lashing it unstoppably home. For a split second Davie thinks it might be him. He has the ball. He can see the goal. There's nobody between him and it. But he hesitates. The tackle's brutal. He goes down and his head reels and he sees stars and when the pain kicks in he thinks his ankle must be broken. He lies there in agony and sees Leonard Hall blast the ball past the keeper into the net.

'Sorry, pal,' says somebody, a skinny kid Davie's never seen before. Must be the one that tackled him.

'You OK?' says the tackler.

Davie grits his teeth, rubs his ankle.

'Aye,' he says. 'Nae bother.'

As the skinny kid turns to go back to the game, Davie asks,

'You haven't seen Zorro Craig, have you?'

'No,' says the kid. 'And if I did, I'd make sure I was going the other way.'

And off he goes, yelling for the ball.

The dog is standing over Davie, hanging its stupid head over him. Long strings of drool dangle and drip from its gob. Davie reels in disgust, stands up, tries to put some weight on his ankle. Not broken. Very sore. The game surges on towards the far end of the field. Davie waves, tries to catch Raymond's attention, but he's gone.

Davie limps back towards where he'd come from.

The soreness fades.

The laughter and yelling of the teams fade.

He attempts a little run. *Yes, everything's OK*, he thinks. He walks forward, upward. He heads towards the poppies that are shining not far above.

The dog at his side is exhausted.

'Lie down,' he tells it.

It keeps on coming.

'Die,' he tells it.

'I'm sorry,' he tells it. 'No, don't die. Just give up.'

It doesn't die. It doesn't give up. Davie crouches

down and stares into its eyes. He wonders if there's anything in there. He wonders if there's any soul in there. The dog gazes back. Does it wonder the same things about Davie? Is it capable of wondering?

'What are you?' says Davie. He knows the answer would be, 'I am a dog,' but he wants more than that.

'What do you see?' he says. 'What do you think, dog?'

No answer, of course.

'Why are you with me?' he asks.

No answer, just a slobber and a drool and a dangling string of horrid spit.

Then there's music that draws his attention from the stupid dog. A voice, the sound of a violin.

Shona Doonan and her brother, Vincent, are sitting in long grass, leaning against an allotment fence. Davie waves at Shona and she waves back and Vincent fiddles and she goes on singing some ancient song.

He goes higher.

He sits for a moment among the astonishing poppies. He falls back and lies among them. They have no scent but the air seems filled with their intensity, and seems to glow. He breathes in this warm poppy air, takes it deep into himself, imagines that the air inside his lungs is red, that the redness spreads and seeps through all of him.

He closes his eyes. He breathes so deep. The pain in his ankle relents as he breathes. He could sleep here, find himself drifting easily into strange red dreams. But he is so dry. He sits up again and takes out Oliver Henderson's pear from the sack and he begins to eat. It's battered and bruised and soft and delicious but far from enough. He needs to drink.

So stupid, not to have brought something to drink on such a day as this.

He knows where there's water higher up, beyond the zigzag path, beyond the kissing gate. He'll reach it soon enough.

He takes out his book.

He draws Shona and her brother, she in bright red, he in bright green.

He draws musical notes the way Fernando Craig drew his frightened cry. The notes leap and curl and swarm from their mouths and bodies and from the violin, and they rise through the shimmering red–blue Tyneside air towards the larks.

And then his name is called from what must be so far away.

'Davie! Davie! Davie!'

He looks back down towards the field.

Gosh Todd, running on to the green from the allotment path. He must be able to see Davie. He swings his arms wide and goes on calling the name, his voice so tiny it might be from a different world.

'Davie! Davie! Davie! Stop, Davie!'

Davie doesn't want to be with Gosh Todd. He stands up and pretends he doesn't see, doesn't hear. He walks on. After a time he turns back to see if Gosh is following. No. The footballers swarm around him, and he's absorbed by them, lost in them, and he runs with them across the green and empty spaces towards the far-off goals.

THIRTEEN

The zigzag path. It starts beyond the poppies. It follows the route of an ancient stream. Sometimes the water gushes and pours, this summer it's a thin elusive trickle. Davie looks with longing at the water, but he knows it could be perilous. Who knows what dead things might be lying in it further up? The path weaves back and forth past ruined cottages. In places the banks are higher than your head. There's shrubs and long grass and stunted trees and huge boulders and stones and tangled brambly gardens. He's been here so often in his short life. He's made dens here, lit fires here, played Cops and Robbers, Cowboys and Indians, and Japs and English here. He's seen toads and rats and grass snakes. He knows tales of kids bitten by adders here.

Last summer, he spent nights camping out here with

Gosh Todd and other pals. One day, they all stripped off most of their clothes, daubed themselves with mud, pretended that they were feral children, brought up in the wilderness with wild beasts. They had no parents, no schooling, no power of speech. They spent the day grunting, howling, lumbering about on all fours. When they did use words, they muttered that this was how they'd really like to be, this was the life they'd really like to live. They screamed the names of teachers, policemen and priests and yelled about how they'd torture them and inflict slow and painful deaths. When people passed by they hid in the shrubs and the undergrowth and grunted and hissed and held back their sniggers. Late in the day, somebody somehow killed a rabbit and they skinned it, gutted it, cooked it on a fire. It wasn't properly cooked. Blood trickled down their chins as they ripped the meat from the bones.

All night long, while the full moon shone down on to the walls of the little tent, they told stories of demons, ghosts, and monsters. One of the boys, a shy and skinny kid called Steven Brooks, ran out of the tent gasping in fear at two a.m. and ran all the way through the moonlight to his home in Waterloo Place.

This is where some of town's most vicious fights are

fought. Battles between the Killens and the Craigs, duels with sticks and stones set up in school yards or in The Bay Horse. Maybe Jimmy Killen and Zorro Craig have battled here. Maybe here the blow was struck or the words were said that led each of them to say that they wanted the other dead.

The zigzag path. It's also the place where lads and lasses walk hand in hand. Hand in hand they leave the path and find soft pockets of turf, clearings in the shrubs, where they can lie down with each other, love each other.

It's a place, like all the places that he passes through today, all the places he has passed through since he was an infant, that seeps deep into Davie's dreams. It's a place, like all the places, that feeds the tales he writes, that infects the sentences and pages that fall from his pen as day comes to a close and night comes slowly on.

He walks through everything today as if through a dream, as if through an unfolding tale. It's a tale of exploration, even though he walks through spaces he knows so well. It's a tale in which each step is a word leading him further into the unknown.

Today the zigzag path is deserted. He weaves upward

all alone, only the dog before him, across the almost dried-out stream.

And then he hears a voice in his ear.

'Hello, Davie.'

It brings him to a halt.

A voice so soft, so true, just like his dead father's voice.

Davie looks around, but there's nothing, no one.

He walks on. The voice continues.

'I always loved the zigzag path, Davie.'

Davie walks on. The voice continues.

'Always felt it was leading me somewhere special, somewhere strange. I felt that when I was a lad.'

Davie walks on. The voice continues.

'I felt it when I used to walk up here with you.'

Davie pauses, remembering the days he'd walk up here with Dad, wandering together.

'You felt it too?' says the voice.

'Yes,' Davie whispers and he knows he feels it again today.

'I love you, son.'

Davie blinks the tears from his eyes.

'Walk on in peace, son.'

And then the voice is gone, and there's just the

sound of the larks and the breeze in the grass, and Davie thinks it must not have been there at all, and he leaves the zigzag path and the stream behind and he approaches the kissing gate and he steps into it while the dog slopes through the wizened hawthorn hedge beside it and suddenly here she comes, from the other side, with her black hair flying, the running lass.

FOURTEEN

The earth trembles with the beating of her feet. She's in blue jeans, blue top, black running shoes. A multi-coloured necklace swings and sparkles around her throat. She runs towards the gate, doesn't see Davie there at first, and then she does. She pauses on the other side. She leans forward, gasping for breath. Her voice wavers.

'Do you know Zorro Craig?' she says.

'Aye,' says Davie.

'Have you seen him?'

'No.'

He's seen her at school, he's seen her at the park. Maria. Maria O'Flynn. Slender and bright-eyed.

She waves her arm towards the world behind her.

'Been looking everywhere. There's so much space

up here, so many places he could be. He could be anywhere.'

She stands up straight and looks at him.

'Do you know what they say he's done?' she says.

'Yes.'

'Do you believe it?' she says.

'I don't know. I don't know what to believe.'

'Nor me.'

She comes closer to the gate. She peers at him.

'You're called Davie, aren't you?' she says. 'Hello, Davie.'

'Hello, Maria.'

'It was me.'

'What was you?'

'It was me they fought about. I was with Jimmy and I chucked him. Then I was with Zorro and they started battling about me so I chucked Zorro too. I'm just an ordinary lass. I don't want any of it. I want an ordinary life. What's happening down below?'

'There's lots of police. The Craigs and Killens are getting ready to fight again.'

She sighs and groans.

'So stupid. It was me and it wasn't me. It was nothing to do with me.'

Davie stands within the kissing gate and looks at her.

'Why you telling me?' he says.

'Because you're here. Because there's nobody else to tell up here.'

He thinks of Paddy Kelly. He thinks of love.

He may as well ask her.

'Did you love them?' he says.

'I liked them. They were both wild but I liked them both.'

The dog stands beyond the gate, looking at Davie, as if asking him to move forward. The hot breeze still presses at Davie's back.

'Did they love you?' says Davie.

'They said they did. They said it mainly after I'd chucked them. Whatever love they had wasn't stronger than the hate they had for each other. It was about me but it wasn't about me. I was nothing to do with it. Love was nothing to do with it. It was about their stupid hate.'

She spreads her arms towards the sky.

'And now poor Jimmy's dead and Zorro's gone. And I think I'm going crazy, Davie. I've been running round up here, yelling for Zorro, then sometimes I find

I'm yelling for Jimmy too, like they're all mixed up in me.'

'You should go back down, go back home.'

'No, not yet. I'll keep on looking.'

'What will you do if you find him?'

'I'll kiss him. Ha! I'll kiss him. I'll tell him he's been stupid and to come back down again with me.'

She looks towards the south.

'I'll look over that way now,' she says.

She steps into the gate before Davie can move through.

She sighs and stands before him with the gate between them.

'We have to kiss before we can go through,' she says.

'What?'

'It's a kissing gate.'

His heart thumps.

'So what?' he says.

She sighs again. She laughs.

'It's stupid,' she says. 'But they say that at every kissing gate there's pixies watching. If they see folk going through the gate without kissing, they'll bring bad luck.'

'What kind of bad luck?'

'Simple things like bad weather or lost money but sometimes terrible things like broken bones. Or like death . . .'

Davie says nothing. His heart thumps faster.

'It's stupid,' she says. 'And it might be nonsense and it might be childish. But we're all still kids, aren't we?'

She leans towards him.

'And we've had quite enough bad luck today. Kiss me, Davie. Please.'

So he leans towards her and their lips touch for an instant, and he steps out again and lets her through and she thanks him and off she runs and he watches her and his soul is reeling.

FIFTEEN

He passes through the gate. He pauses and listens for Dad's voice again but it's not there. The dog walks on in front of him, leads him forward. Perhaps the dog too knows where the water is.

Up here, the town is nearly gone. There are some ancient knocked-down terraced houses, ancient broken garden walls. The ground is all disturbed from ancient mine-workings. There are holes and gouges and cracks in the earth. There are boarded-over and fenced-off pit-shafts. There are turfed pit-heaps and ripped-up rail lines. Soon everything will be gone, grown-over, sunken-down, disappeared. Just uneven stony earth made beautiful with bright green grass, moss and lichen, speedwell, hawthorn and forget-me-nots.

So many places where Zorro could be hiding, so

many places where he could be lost.

Far below are the ancient mining tunnels. Davie might have worked in them had he been born a hundred years ago. Down there are the bodies of boys like him, killed in collapsed tunnels and seams or by explosions. He could have been lost in the earth like them, lost in time like them.

Sometimes he dreams of the pit children. Sometimes he sees them rise from his sleeping mind. They stand and crouch in his bedroom, silent. Sometimes he dreams that he sees them here, sitting at ease on the turf in the sunlight, scrawny children with blackened bodies and glittering eyes allowed out from the dark into the modern peaceful day.

He looks around himself now. He imagines those children here, now. They seem so close. If he could relax in the right way, or slip closer to a state of dreams, or simply open his eyes and see more clearly, he knows that they would be with him, come back from death into this bright Tyneside day. Ghosts and phantoms would become as real as he is for a few short vivid moments, as real as dogs and skylarks here in this strange miraculous world.

He smiles. He looks for pixies and for pit children

and he listens for his father and he looks for Zorro Craig.

Rabbits race for cover as he passes. He sees a mouse flick down into its hole. There are foxes here, badgers. Sometimes deer can be seen to pass this way. There are slow worms, grass snakes. Now the buzzards are much closer: a pair of them, wings outstretched, jagged wingtips silhouetted against the blue.

The dog walks on, leading the way to Cooper's Hole.

So strange. Not many people seem to know about this place. It's nothing huge or special and maybe that explains it. It's tucked away behind some tumbledown shacks. There's a little spring trickling out of a few rocks into a little pond of dark water with wet moss and a few reeds around it and some old stones you can sit on and stare into it. There are a few scraggy hawthorn trees. There's a low stone arch that looks very old, and below that there's a low entrance straight into the dark earth.

It was Dad who first led Davie through the kissing gate and further to this place.

'There's always secret places waiting to be found,' Dad said. 'Even in a little town like this, where you can think you've seen everything there is to see.'

Davie crouches by the spring, cups his hands and lets the icy water make a pool in them. He sips and drinks. So icy, so delicious. He sits on a rock and takes out the coloured pencils and the sketch book again. He inspects the ancient stuff on the pages: stick figures, scribbly drawings of the family, a green drawing of a teddy bear called Spook, a picture of a rocket heading to the moon. The pages are faded, and crisp at the edges. He looks at the pages that he has begun to fill today.

What would lads like Zorro Craig think, seeing him colouring in like a bairn? What would the lasses think? It doesn't matter. Nobody can see. And he thinks of Fernando Craig, the vicious hard lad with the tender voice and the ability to create such beauty with a few swift marks. Fernando Craig, he understands.

He looks at the trickling water. He catches his breath. What he sees is commonplace and wonderful. As the white light of the sun falls through the splashes and the spray, the light is broken up, the colours separate. A rainbow appears and disappears, appears and disappears. The truth within the white light of the sun is shown to him and shown to him.

He laughs out loud, seeing this truth in his childhood tin of coloured pencils. He colours, scribbles and draws. He creates nothing that is recognisable. He allows the colours to roam and spread across the paper. Then he begins to make the marks that try to draw this strange place, Cooper's Hole. He draws grass and water and stone arch and trees. He draws wild flowers and water weed. He draws the bees. He tries to match the colours in the real world with the colours in his book. Impossible, but he goes on doing it. And, entranced by all this, he is cast back to his primary school, to the day Mrs Fagan put a vase of daisies and buttercups in front of the children.

'Take up your pencils,' she said. 'Take up your paints and brushes.'

'But, miss,' someone groaned. 'We've done buttercups before.'

'Not these buttercups,' she said. 'And not on this day and not at the age you are now.'

She moved gently through the class.

'Some artists,' she said, 'spend their whole lives painting the very same thing time and time again.'

'It must get boring, miss,' someone said.

'Oh, no,' she answered. 'Every time you look, every

time you draw, you see something very new.'

She laughed her kindly laugh.

'And some artists,' she said, 'even spend year after year painting pictures of themselves.'

'Is that 'cos they're bigheaded, miss?'

'Oh, no,' she said again. 'They're trying to find out who they are. And they're seeing how they change and grow, day by day, year by year.'

She reached down and touched the petals of a daisy.

'Magical things,' she said. 'Did you know that when the sun is out, the daisy opens wide, and when the sun is gone, the daisy folds in upon itself. That is why they are often called "days' eyes".'

The children painted and drew. They paid attention to their work. Mrs Fagan praised them. She gently helped guide uncertain hands to move brushes and pencils across paper.

'One day,' she said, 'I will find some sunflowers to bring to you. They too are magical. Brilliant yellow things from the far south that follow the sun with their faces as it passes overhead.'

'I've seen them, miss,' said Davie. 'They're in a painting that my dad loves.'

'Ah, yes. Perhaps it's one of the paintings that I love too.'

She tenderly touched his head.

'Colour the world, children,' she said, 'just as that artist coloured the world. Make it beautiful.'

'I can't get it right, miss,' someone muttered. 'It doesn't look how it's supposed to look.'

'Don't worry. It needn't look like any particular thing at all. How could we imagine that we could make a world as perfect and as lovely as the world that God has made? All we can do is to do our best. Paint and draw. Create your own beautiful imperfect world.'

Her voice drifts through the years as Davie cups his hands under the little spring again and sips the icy water again. He squishes it around his mouth, he feels it flowing into him and through him. At his side, the dog drinks too, lowering its mouth into the waters of the pool.

Davie goes on drawing and colouring in the sunlight and the heat, sitting on this rock by Cooper's Hole. He draws Cooper's Hole itself, a gulf of blackness, an entrance to the endless blackness beneath the surface of the earth, black as sleep, black as death. He imagines the blackness of Cooper's Hole deepening and spreading. He is entranced, absorbed, he starts to lose himself again.

He was maybe five years old when he first came here with Dad. They found frogs beneath stones and saw minnows flicker in the water. The minnows flash and flicker still. He creates them on the page with little dashes of white against the water's dark blue. And he tries to catch the impossibly bright sunbeams falling through the hawthorn leaves to sparkle on the water.

Back then, he brought a net and jam jar sometimes, to catch the minnows and carry them home. He'd watch them swimming through their colourless shadowless world on the kitchen windowsill. They never lasted long and he'd feel cruel then. They needed space and freedom, poor things. Who was he to limit their lives like this? But he kept on doing it. Poor innocent long-lost minnows. Poor little dead things.

And now he looks up from his page and his enchantment and he sees that Dad is here.

He shimmers in that light that slants down through the hawthorn trees.

He sits on one of the ancient stones right by Cooper's Hole itself.

He watches Davie, maybe wondering how his son is going to react.

Davie does nothing. Doesn't speak. Keeps very still. Just watches the man who watches him. Sees the colours come and go.

The dog too sits very still, eyes towards the pool.

A frog leaps into the pool and swims across the water in a dead straight line from Davie to his dad. It kicks its legs, and leaves a perfect little wake behind.

Davie quickly draws this blue wake on an empty piece of page.

He considers trying to draw Dad but it seems impossible.

Dad shrugs and smiles.

'So,' he says, just as he used to do to open a conversation.

'So,' answers Davie, just as he used to do.

'So you just out wandering, son?' says Dad.

'Aye.'

'That's good. You always liked that, didn't you?'

'Aye.'

'A grand thing for a lad to do.'

He looks down at the frog, that's now poised right at the water's edge, looking up at him.

'You should never drink the water here. I told you that, didn't I?'

'Aye,' whispers Davie.

'They used to say it turns you daft. They used to say it starts you seeing visions.'

He grins.

'But mebbe that's all bollix. What do you think, son?'

Davie grins back. *Bollix.* The word the priest used, and the word he used to share with Dad when Mam wasn't listening.

'Aye,' he says. 'It's all a load of bollix, Dad.'

'You going far?'

'Dunno. I might do. I think I might be following Zorro Craig.'

'Zorro Craig? Him from Collingwood Terrace?'

'Aye. You've not seen him, have you?'

'No, son. Mind you, I'm not sure I'm really seeing anything at all.'

He's dressed in brown jeans and a green jumper. His blue eyes are bright and kind as ever. He's like he was before he became all shrunken and thin. He turns his eyes to the larks singing high above then looks back and he smiles again.

'Beautiful,' he whispers, just like he used to do.

'This is what it's all about,' he says, just like he used to do.

He laughs at himself saying that, then he asks,

'So why the interest in Zorro Craig?'

'There's talk he might have killed somebody.'

'Killed? Killed who?'

'Jimmy Killen.'

'Jimmy bliddy *Killen*?'

'Aye. It's true. I've seen the body. I've seen the knife.'

'What the hell's he doing killing *him*?'

'I dunno, Dad. It's all a mystery, Dad.'

He laughs at that as well. It's what they always said when they got to something that seemed beyond them. *It's all a mystery. It's all beyond our comprehension.*

'Killing!' says Dad. 'What's anybody doing killing anybody? There's enough death in the world without the Zorro Craigs adding to it all. Isn't that right, son?'

'Yes.'

Then a thought comes into Davie's mind.

'You've not seen Jimmy, have you?' he says.

'Can't say I have.' Dad grins. 'Mind you, that could depend on how long the lad's been dead.'

Then he just looks at Davie and Davie just looks back at him, and the time they spend in doing that seems to last an hour, a day, a life, an eternity.

'You'll be all right,' says Dad at last. 'Keep on wandering out here in these lovely places on this lovely day. You're a good lad. No harm'll come to you up here.'

The dog licks the pool, its long tongue dangling down into the water. Dad smiles.

'What's with the dog?' he says.

Davie rolls his eyes.

'I can't stand the thing,' he mutters. 'I can't get rid of it.'

Dad grins.

'Mebbe it's looking after you,' he says.

'It's not. Go away,' Davie whispers to the dog. 'Go on. Get lost.'

The dog just stares back at him, stupid. It licks water from the pool.

'You'll be all right,' says Dad again. 'Don't worry, son.'

When Davie looks back to where Dad was, he's gone. There's just the pond, the spring, the colours, the archway and the dark entrance to the earth. Davie isn't disturbed. It seems to be the way that things should be. He sighs. Cooper's Hole. They used to wonder if it led down to the ancient coal mines below, whether it was the start of a tunnel that would take you right through to the other side of the hill, or whether it was the entrance to Hell itself.

'No way of knowing,' Dad once said, 'without crawling in and finding it all out for yourself. And I don't intend to do that. Do you?'

'Not likely,' said Davie.

He stares at the dark entrance. Maybe that's where Dad came out from. Maybe that's where he's gone back into.

With a black pencil, Davie makes the hole seem even darker, deeper, more dangerous, then he wonders if Zorro Craig is finding out for himself and using the place as a hide-out. He could hole up in there by day and come out raiding shops and people's kitchens at night. Davie peers harder, strains his eyes, like he might see the shape of Zorro Craig, or see his eyes staring out of the dark. But, no, it's all too wet in there, all too confined. Zorro will have travelled much further on if he's got any sense. He'll be putting miles between himself and the murder scene.

Davie puts two white dots on the black for Zorro's staring eyes.

He thinks about writing a horror story called *The Monster of Cooper's Hole.*

He thinks about writing a story about a father coming back from death, but knows it would be impossible without it seeming barmy, scary, far too full with weeping, far too sentimental.

He simply writes, in a green pencil.

Dad came back today at Cooper's Hole, just for a little while.

He draws the frog. It's now right where Dad was. The skin under its mouth is lifting and falling. It sits there above the water on the rock and it's shiny and green and really beautiful.

Davie sits there for a long time. Images from his infancy move through him as the earth turns and sun above him follows its arching route across the sky. The images flow through his mind and body and down into his arm and hand and make their marks and fill the lovely empty sketch book pages.

The slobbering of the dog brings him out of it. He curses it, but he closes his book and puts the pencils and the book back into the sack.

He takes another sip of cool clear water from the spring.

The frog suddenly leaps into the pool and disappears.

Shimmering damselflies dance there.

'Shove off,' he tells the dog.

But it takes no notice. It stands waiting for him to follow, and it pads along ahead of him as he leaves Cooper's Hole and wanders on.

SIXTEEN

The hill steepens towards the crest. There's a point where it's possible to stand on a high bare rock and look back to see what's gone before. Davie stands there. Below him are the paths and the playing fields, the disturbed earth, the zigzag path, the poppies, the town. He seems to have come so far but it's all there, all still visible, all just a short walk away. He sees the steeple of the church and he sees again dead Jimmy Killen and the bloody knife lying together in the rubble. It already seems a hundred miles away, a hundred years ago, but the place is small and the time's been short. The smallness and the shortness are so strange in their immensity.

He sees the swarming footballers, like a distant flock of earthbound birds. And apart from them he sees someone tiny, dressed in bright red, coming up through the green fields. It must be Shona Doonan. She waves her arms in wide circles just like Gosh did. Davie shuts his eyes and listens and he swears he can hear her voice, calling his name as if it's a song.

'Davie! Davie! Come back, Davie!'

And he wants to call to her, wants to see her coming up the zigzag path to him. But she's so, so distant and he might be wrong. She might be simply singing, she might be calling someone else's name. She shimmers in the light and heat, a bright red dot in all that great green land.

Still the breeze blows upward, into Davie's face. It plays across his skin. He sees how far the sun has moved. He sees the buzzards drifting in the blue above. He hears the larks and sees the tiny dark dots of them. *Are they scared of buzzards?* he wonders. *Does it trouble them that they share the same sky?*

Then there's shouting nearby. It comes from just across the ridge. A man's voice, crying out.

'Get off, you stupid thing!'

There's a touch on Davie's shoulder.

'I'd better go now,' comes Dad's whisper.

Davie looks around but there's nothing.

'Goodbye, son,' comes Dad's whisper.

'Goodbye, Dad,' whispers his son.

And he listens, but there's no more, just the raucous voice again.

'Begone, you stupid thing!'

Davie walks across the ridge.

SEVENTEEN

It's Wilf Pew. How the hell did he get here? He's hopping about and doing something with his legs. The long coat's swirling about him.

He sees Davie.

'Stop just standing there,' he says. 'Do something useful and give us a hand with this damn leg, will you?'

He topples over into the grass under a hawthorn tree.

'How did you get here?' says Davie.

'What? How did I get here?'

'Yes.'

'What kind of question's that? I came out of me mammy's tummy, just like you.'

'No. I mean how did you get up the hill?'

'I flew. I grew wings and took flight. How do you

think I got here? I walked. While you were dreaming down by Cooper's Hole, I belted past you.'

'I didn't see you.'

'So now you only believe in things you can see for yourself?'

'No. So you saw me?'

'Of course I blimmin' saw you.'

'Did you see anything else?'

'What do you mean, did I see anything else? Of course I did. I saw the whole wide blimmin' world. Or mebbe you think there's only you in it and nothing else.'

'I don't.'

'Good! So can you see this leg? Good! Now get over here and give us a hand with it.'

He wriggles and squirms and grunts. He starts shoving the top of his trousers down. He's doing something with buckles and belts inside the trousers.

'Stupid thing!' he says. 'Supposed to liberate us but it just gets in the bliddy way. Pull that foot, lad.'

'Eh?'

'Pull that foot.' He points to his right foot. 'What's wrong with you lot these days? Get hold of that foot and pull.'

So Davie kneels down and grabs Wilf's foot in both hands. There's a thick leather shoe on it. The dog's staring at the foot and drooling.

'Now!' says Wilf. 'Pull the thing!'

Davie tugs the foot. Nothing happens.

'Where's your strength?' says Wilf. 'Pull the bugger.'

Davie leans back. He pulls hard and the foot starts to slide out of the trousers. There's a hard bright pink leg coming out with it. Davie has to stop. He can't go on. When he was a kid, he used to wonder what Wilf's leg was like. Now he doesn't want to know. It's like being in a horror movie.

'Go on,' says Wilf. 'It won't bite you. Pull!'

Davie pulls again. The foot and the leg keep on sliding out of the trousers. It gets tighter and slower as the leg gets thicker at the thigh.

'Pull!' says Wilf. 'Yo-o, heave ho!'

Davie pulls, and with a final jerk the whole leg comes out of the trousers and he falls back into the grass with the foot still in his hands.

'Good lad!' says Wilf. 'I knew you had it in you.'

He puffs and blows and groans.

'That is bliddy heaven,' he sighs.

He rubs his hip.

Davie sits up and dares to look. The leg's horrible. Long and pink and stiff with leather straps and buckles at the top of it. It's gleaming in the light.

'Just look at that blimmin' monstrosity,' says Wilf. 'How'd you like one of them to get about on, lad?'

'I wouldn't, Mr Pew.'

'Too damn right, you wouldn't!'

The dog starts licking the leg and dribbling drool on it. Davie thinks he's going to be sick.

'Get off me leg, ye daft dog!' says Wilf.

He kicks at it with his good leg.

'What the hell is Foulmouth doing with you?' he says.

'Foulmouth? Who's Foulmouth?'

'That damn dog, of course! He's been pestering me for days and now he's got the two of us.'

'Why's he called Foulmouth?'

'What kind of question's that? Have you not caught a whiff of his gob? Gerroff, you stupid dog!'

The dog backs off.

'Anyway,' says Wilf, 'we're getting sorted out, aren't we? Next thing is, you got any food in that sack of yours?'

Davie thinks about the bara brith from this morning.

He doesn't really want to share it with Wilf Pew.

'No,' he says.

He suddenly realises how hungry he is. He should have got three pies, not just two.

'I had some pies,' he says. 'But I ate them.'

'Typical! Never mind. There's still a fruit gum or two. And we'll pick up something as we wend our way onwards.'

Davie says nothing. Wend their way to where? And does Wilf mean they'll be wending their way together? And how the hell will he do any wending at all on a single leg?

He must know what Davie's thinking. He reaches into the long grass and lifts up a branch that's lying under the tree. He strips the leaves from it. He snaps off the thorns. It's nearly as long as he is. There's a V-shaped joint at the top of it.

'This is all a bloke needs,' he says. 'Help us up, lad.'

He reaches out towards Davie.

Davie doesn't move.

'You're not very quick, are you?' he says. 'I asked you to help us up.'

So Davie gets up and takes Wilf's hand. It feels really strong and really cold. Wilf levers his way up till he's standing on one foot.

'Now the branch,' he says.

So Davie gets the branch and Wilf takes it and leans on it, resting his armpit in the V-shaped joint. He stands there grinning, half-silhouetted against the western sky.

'See?' he says. 'Nature will provide.'

The empty trouser leg flaps gently in the breeze.

'This is the life!' he says. 'Put that leg in the tree so we know where to pick it up on the way back.'

He just looks at Davie and waits when the boy doesn't move.

So Davie pushes the dog aside and lifts the leg. It's heavy and horrible. It's hollow. He reaches right up and shoves it down thigh-first over a hawthorn branch and the leg hangs there, horizontal, with the belt and buckles dangling and with the black shoe pointing towards the sky, like some weird new branch in a weird old tale.

'Beautiful!' says Wilf.

And when Davie steps back to look at it properly, he has to think the same.

'Onward!' says Wilf.

'Where to?'

'To wherever you want to go!' he says. 'To find whatever it is you're looking for!'

'I don't know where I want to go. I don't know what I'm looking for.'

'Kids today!' he says.

'Blokes today!' Davie snaps back at him.

Wilf does a little jig on branch and his single leg.

'Good lad!' He laughs. 'Well said! Bliddy blokes today!'

Davie groans. He wants to stop right here. He wants to just head home again.

'Follow me!' says Wilf.

'What? Where to?'

'How the hell should I know?'

He limps and lollops away.

And Davie finds himself following Wilf Pew and the dog, over the hill and into a land he's seen a hundred times before.

EIGHTEEN

'It's somewhere down below,' says Wilf.

'What is?'

'What do you mean, what is? Me leg, of course. What else do you think we're talking about?'

'Dunno. I didn't think we were talking about anything.'

'Well, no, but you must have been wondering. Everybody gets to wondering. Were you not?'

'Not really, Mr Pew.'

'Have you got no curiosity, lad?'

Davie says nothing. There's nothing to say to that.

'Obviously not,' he says. 'But I'll tell you, anyway. It's down below. A long way down below.'

'Ah,' says Davie.

What the hell am I doing here? he wonders.

Foulmouth slobbers, maybe wondering the same thing.

'Aye,' says Wilf. 'I was a pitman, you see, a long way down below and the roof came crashing in on me one day. On me leg, anyway.'

'Ah,' says Davie.

'Aye. I thought I was a goner and me pals thought I was a goner, but once the dust had settled the doc came and sawed it off right there and then. You ever had a leg sawed off right there and then?'

Davie sighs and shakes his head.

'Thought not. But you can imagine it, can't you? Can't you? He chopped it off and they brung me up to the light again. I'd given up and then I'm brung back up all safe and sound. It was like rising up to Heaven, son. It was like they'd given us a pair of wings.'

'That's good.'

'*Good*? It was blimmin' . . . transcendental, son!'

'I thought you must have lost it in the war.'

'See? You have been wondering! Aye, there's many a one that thinks it was war till they're telt about the happenings deep down below. You sure you've got no grub? I'm clamming.'

'No,' Davie lies.

'OK. You any good at killing rabbits? We could cook it on a fire.'

'No.'

'Typical! Anyway, it liberated us.'

'What did?'

'Getting me leg chopped off, of course! It was the end of the pit for me. It was the end of going deep down below. I was footloose and free, the world me oyster.'

'Did you get another job?'

'Aye. I became an Olympic sprinter.'

Davie sighs.

'We could eat the dog, I suppose,' says Wilf.

Davie looks at the dog. He tries hard not to imagine eating it.

'You ever eaten a dog?' says Wilf.

Davie say nothing.

'Take no notice,' Wilf says. 'I'm rambling. The more important question is, what's the point of it all?'

'The point of it all?'

'Aye. What we doing? Where we going? Why are we here?'

'I don't know, Mr Pew.'

'Nor do I, son. Nor do I. I've lived a thousand years and I'm none the wiser.'

He groans deeply.

'Ah, well,' he mutters. 'The least we can do is wander on towards the setting of the sun.'

NINETEEN

The land slopes away before them. Paddocks and fields and hedges and copses. The metallic river stretching westward between its banks towards dark moors. The towns on the banks, the places he knows, Blaydon, Newburn, Wylam. Other settlements far away. The city to the north, Newcastle, the arch of its bridge, its rooftops and steeples and office blocks and apartment blocks. And then the northward-stretching land, the great plain of Northumberland and the bulges of the dark Cheviots.

Wilf Pew lunges onward.

Davie walks at his side.

The dog lopes, gasping.

Davie is parched again. He relives the moments of drinking at Cooper's Hole and his body yearns for water.

He's seen this land a hundred times before, but it's never looked like this. Here beyond the crest there is no breeze at all. The yellow sun is on its way towards the west and still pours down its light and heat. Davie's skin is hot. Everything is baked. Everything is scorched to stillness.

Apart from Davie, Wilf and Foulmouth, nothing seems to move. Only the bees that drone from bloom to bloom in the hedges and the grass to dip into the sweetness there. Only the flies, the silent butterflies. Only the singing larks and the buzzards high up that elegantly wheel across the blue.

Davie sees that the blue of the sky is the blue of a bird's egg.

For a moment he sees the world as an egg, the sky as the shell.

Everything inside the shell is gloopy, changing, growing.

Wings will be forming, he thinks. *Then a beak will chip at the shell, making an exit to an undiscovered unimagined world beyond.*

He stares at the sky.

What is the undiscovered unimagined world beyond the sky?

'I went there!' Wilf Pew suddenly announces.

Davie draws his attention back to his companion.

He tries to lick his lips.

'Where?' he says.

Wilf balances on his one leg and points northward with his hawthorn crutch.

'There!' he says. 'The blimmin' Cheviots and then beyond. I was liberated by the chopped-off leg. I could do owt in the world I wanted to. So I slung a sack on me back and I left me hearth and home and headed north.'

He lowers the crutch and leans on it.

'That's where Edinburgh is,' he says. 'Past them distant mountains.'

'Aye,' says Davie. 'I know.'

'You been there?'

'Where?'

'Edinburgh.'

'No.'

'Then how do you know it's there at all?'

Davie sighs.

'I just do,' he says. 'I've read about it. I've seen it on the telly.'

'On the telly! What kind of knowing's that? I come

back home and they said, "Where ye been, Wilf?" And I said, "I walked to Edinburgh." And they said, "But, Wilf, you've only got one blimmin' leg." And I said, "What's that got to do with the price of fish?" It was nice, Edinburgh. You should get yourself there. With your young legs it'd only take a week or so to walk.'

Davie wonders about such a walk. He can imagine the pleasure of walking through the fields, alongside the rivers and over the hills and into the city. He wonders about the best routes but he doesn't ask Wilf about them. He doesn't want to encourage him.

'You could,' says Wilf. 'It's just a matter of getting started and keeping on. Like most things are. And folk were kind. They gave us milk and pies. Horses eat grass.'

'What?'

'And they look fit enough,' says Wilf. 'You ever tried it?'

'No.'

Wilf swivels on the crutch and drops to the ground. He rips up some blades of grass from the side of the path. He shoves them into his mouth and starts to chew. He chews for a while, then spits it all out again.

'It's canny,' he says to Davie. 'You should try it, son.'

Davie sees the green juice at the corners of Wilf's mouth. He sees the green stains on his teeth.

Davie's so tired. Again, he has thoughts of turning back, going home. And his mind is turning to Knickerbocker Specials, Molly Myers' pies, football with the lads, and to Shona Doonan's face.

'Stop dreaming,' Wilf says. 'Do something useful and help us up.'

Davie doesn't move.

He wants to lie down. He wants to go back. He imagines he can hear Shona and Gosh.

'Davie! Davie! Come back, Davie!'

'Do it,' says Wilf. He reaches out to Davie. 'Please!'

So Davie reaches out. Wilf grasps his hand, and swivels up to stand again. He groans.

Suddenly, Wilf looks ancient. He sighs deeply. His eyes are clouded. His head hangs forward. He grits his teeth and grimaces as he leans upon the hawthorn crutch.

'Mebbe I should turn it to a ladder,' he says.

'Turn what to a ladder?'

Wilf groans and grimaces again. He shuts his eyes.

There's sweat on his brow.

'This crutch, son,' he says. 'I'm tired. Mebbe I should turn it to a ladder and climb me way to Heaven at last.'

'I think I should . . .' starts Davie. 'I think it's time . . .'

'Aye,' says Wilf. 'I know, son. It soon gets late.'

He reaches out and cups Davie's chin in his hand and stares into his eyes.

'You'll be all right, lad,' he says. 'I walked to blimmin' Edinburgh and back. The least you can do is wend a little further with Wilf Pew.'

He sighs.

'Please, lad,' he says.

'I'm no danger to you, you know,' he says.

Davie turns his eyes from Wilf, looks into the world again. Soon, everything will change. New shades will seep into the single intense blue of the sky. Reds and oranges, yellows and greys. It'll just be the turning of the day again, the coming on of dusk and night again. Davie's seen it a thousand times, but there's never been a day like this before.

Wilf taps Davie's shoulder, gently.

'Don't worry, lad,' he says. 'We'll get you there and back again before the night comes on.'

'Get me where?' says Davie.

'Don't ask me. But it looks like Foulmouth knows. Maybe we're already here.'

Davie hesitates.

Wilf digs into his pocket. He holds out the fluffy packet of fruit gums.

Davie takes one, a red one.

He lifts it up to the sun to see the red brilliance of it, then puts it into his mouth.

'Good lad,' says Wilf. 'That'll keep you going for a little bit.'

It's so sweet and delicious on the tongue. Davie sighs. And Foulmouth lopes a little further, along a lane where the grass is scorched, across a rough paddock with a black-and-white pony in it, through a scant hedgerow, then another where the birds are singing brightly, across a drift of buttercups and forget-me-nots, and leads them to where the land rises to its highest point, towards an intensity of yellow, as if the earth is burning, shining, offering light back to the blazing sun.

TWENTY

It's a great sloping patch of yellow gorse. The air above is yellow, yellow is the earth below. There's a pathway through the gorse. Wilf Pew comes to a halt before it, leaning on his crutch. The dog sits down on the pathway. Davie passes them both and goes deeper into the yellow heat. The shrubs are higher than Davie's head. He sways to keep his body away from the vicious spelks and spines. He hears pops and crackles, small explosions. He sees that the dark seed pods of the gorse are bursting in the heat. The black and tiny seeds are scattered through the yellow air. He sees a hundred thousand black-and-yellow bees that dip into yellow flower after yellow flower. He hears their buzz, their drone, their whine. The ground is dry and dusty, carpeted with fallen petals, seeds and spines. In here the day is even brighter, even stiller, even hotter. The yellow air is thick. Davie breathes the yellowness of gorse into himself. There is a yellow smell of coconut. All alone, he gasps for yellow breath. He reels with exhaustion, thirst, the heat.

He hardly knows what he is doing. He doesn't know why he is doing it. He opens the haversack and takes out the fox mask. He pulls it over his head. It's too small, too tight, it's made for little children, but he pulls it hard until his face is a fox face and he stares out through fox eyes. He bares his teeth, he snarls, he yelps a fox yelp. He pads through the yellow shrubs. He begins to lose himself. He breathes fox breath, he feels fox blood running through his veins.

He is fox, he is wild. He prowls through the yellow gorse.

He staggers, totters. He rips the fox mask off. Now he takes the antlers and sets them on his head. They're frail and plastic things that slip as he tries to get them to stay put. He holds them in place as he moves deer-like through the gorse, until they begin to be part of him, until they begin to be antlers growing from his own skull, until he loses himself and is no longer Davie. He feels the deer heart beating in his chest. He feels dense coarse deer hair growing on his skin.

He is deer, he is wild.

Amid the gorse and the bees and the exploding seed pods, below the blue sky and the yellow sun and upon the blazing earth, he loses himself, finds the fox and the deer inside himself, and he is wild.

He staggers, totters, falls.

He pulls the antlers off, throws them down.

At the heart of the gorse patch, a strip of black rock grained with silvery threads is exposed. He crawls to it, lies down upon it. It is hot. There is a shallow depression in the rock, shaped as if to accept him. All around, it is as if the yellowness is pouring out from the earth into the sky. It is as if the earth has opened, as if the golden light contained within the earth is offered up to the golden sun.

Davie is at the summit of the town. He is balanced on the surface of the earth. He rests upon the hot black rock and the yellow light. He stares towards the buzzards of the eggshell sky. There is nothing but the buzzards between himself and the sun. He drifts, he swoons. He shuts his eyes. He feels that the earth is pressing him upward, that it is offering him to the sky, that he has lost all weight, and that he could rise into the yellow air and disappear.

And then here are the claws at his shoulders. Here's the turmoil of the air caused by the beating wings above. Here is the buzzard's single high-pitched short cry. He does not dare to look. He is lifted up. He dangles from the buzzard's claws, is carried upward by the buzzard's beating wings. He flies upward through the skylarks.

And at last he opens his eyes and dares to look.

He is in the air, dangling from the buzzard's claws. The song of skylarks is all around him. And below him, that's where he comes from. The yellow gorse and then the hill and then the zigzag path and then the playing fields and then his little town. And the river running through the towns towards the distant sea. And the city and the suburbs and factories and churches. The shipyards with half-built ships. Factories belching fumes and din. And the curved earth stretching away from this heart. Northumberland and Durham and distant Cumberland. Everything exposed by the gift of this summer day's intense and lovely light. Everything seen by a boy dangling from a buzzard's claws. And Davie stretches out his arms and spreads his fingers and gives a short, sharp high-pitched cry, a buzzard's cry of liberty and joy.

And then is dropped back down on to the black rock in the yellow gorse.

And he lies there.

Sun falls towards the west.

And the light turns.

Eggshell blue is touched with drifts of red.

And Davie sleeps a kind of sleep.

TWENTY-ONE

And doesn't see the boy who walks into the gorse. Doesn't see the tall and slender one dressed in blue and black – blue jeans and black denim shirt with pearlised buttons on it. Black pointed elastic-sided boots. There's dried blood on his cheek. Blood has trickled down from beneath his cuffs and dried on the smooth skin of his hand. He's a bonny boy. Smooth cheeks, shining eyes.

The first Davie knows of it is when the slender boy crouches at his side and gently touches Davie's shoulder.

'Kid,' he says softly. 'Kid. Are you all right, kid?'

Davie imagines that he is at home, in his bed, the only place where he ever sleeps. But he's confused to hear a voice close by him that is not the voice of his mother, nor, until so recently, that of his father.

Confused to feel the touch that is not of his mother or father.

'Kid,' says the slender boy again. 'Kid. Wake up, kid.'

Davie comes out of his dreamless sleep. Opens his eyes. Sees the black elastic-sided boots, the blue jeans, the pearlised buttons on the black shirt. Sees the blood. Sees the face. Wonders if he's dreaming, as if sleep is boring emptiness and waking is the vivid dream.

'Zorro Craig,' he says.

'The same,' says the boy. 'And who are you? And what the hell you doing here?'

Davie closes his eyes again a moment, remembers the buzzard, its wings, its claws. He doesn't know how to answer. He wonders if he is the same boy who was lifted into the sky, or if he is some other boy, some other Davie, carried here from a different place.

'I thought you were dead,' says Zorro. 'You looked just like you were dead.'

Davie squirms on the rock. He tries to sit up. Zorro helps him, holding his arm.

'You got anything to drink?' says Davie.

'Aye,' says Zorro. 'I've got a little bit. Was keeping it for later but I guess you're the one in need.'

He takes a glass bottle of Coca-Cola from his pocket and passes it to Davie. It's a third full. Davie unscrews the cap and swigs. The liquid's warm – the heat of the day, the heat of Zorro's body. Its fizz has gone but it's wet and sweet, it's delicious.

'Drink up,' says Zorro. 'Gan on. I see you need it more than me.'

Davie sits up on the rock and swigs. He feels his body relaxing as the liquid enters it. He tastes the Coca-Cola and knows that he is tasting Zorro Craig too. He feels himself coming properly awake.

'Thank you,' he says.

He looks to the pathways. No sign of Foulmouth, no sign of Wilf Pew. The sun has moved further, fallen further.

'What you doing up here?' says Zorro.

'I came from down below. I was just wandering.'

'Bliddy wandering?'

'Aye.'

'I've seen ye before,' says Zorro. 'What's yer name?'

'Davie,' says Davie.

He sees the fox mask and the antlers on the dusty earth. Discarded children's toys. He starts to wonder if he should be scared, if he should jump up and run but he feels like he could hardly move.

'Why did you kill Jimmy Killen?' he finds himself saying.

'What?' says Zorro.

'Why did you kill Jimmy?'

'Who telt you I killed Jimmy?'

'I saw him,' says Davie. 'I saw him lying dead in the rubble where the church hall used to be.'

'How could that be?' says Zorro. 'He can't be dead.'

'I saw the knife,' says Davie. 'I saw the blood.'

Zorro takes a cigarette from a packet and lights it with a match struck on the rock.

He breathes in smoke and exhales smoke.

'The police were there,' says Davie. 'And the doctor. And the priest.'

'The bliddy *priest*?'

'Aye.'

'Making sure he gets took straight up to Heaven, aye?'

'I suppose so.'

Zorro groans and smokes his cigarette.

In the distance, a siren wails.

'I heard that earlier,' says Zorro. 'I never thought it'd be for me.'

'It is,' says Davie, and he finds himself saying, 'You'll never get away. Maybe you should let me take you in.'

Zorro snorts.

'Where do you think we are? Texas? You got a shotgun in yer sack?'

Davie imagines crossing the square with Zorro at his side. He imagines handcuffs joining their wrists together. He imagines that he does have a shotgun and walks behind Zorro and points it at the back of his head. He imagines the townsfolk in the streets and in the square applauding as he brings the killer in.

He laughs at the image.

Maybe Zorro imagines the same. He laughs out loud. And the laughter echoes around the gorse patch and suddenly Davie realises how scared he should be. He thinks of his mother. She'll be terrified. Her son is off wandering all alone and there's a killer on the loose. He jumps to his feet.

'What's up with ye?' says Zorro.

'I got to get back,' says Davie. 'Me mam'll be frantic.'

'Frantic?'

''Cos there's a killer on the loose.'

'Aye, there is,' Zorro says. 'And the killer says hold your horses. It's not five minutes since you looked to be at the point of death yourself. You'll do yourself a mischief.'

Davie tries to tug away but Zorro holds him back.

'You going to kill me too?' Davie says.

Zorro leans close. He stares straight into Davie's eyes.

'Aye!' he says. 'That's what killers do. They start with one and get a taste for it and end up killing multitudes.'

He pulls Davie close.

'Do you think that's true?' he says. 'Do you think I've set out on a path with no return?'

Davie looks back into the killer's eyes.

He has no answers.

Zorro pushes him away.

'This is mad,' he says.

He tugs his black shirt and his buttons pop like seed pods as they open.

'You can run if you want to, Davie,' he says. 'But, look, I'm the one that should be dead.'

TWENTY-TWO

Zorro strips off his shirt. There's dark down on his chest. His skin is pale. There's a wound on his upper left arm with a track of dried blood below it.

'This is where the knife struck,' says Zorro.

'Jimmy stabbed you?'

'Aye.'

'Then you stabbed him.'

'No. There was just one knife. There was just one wound. The blood on Jimmy must have come from me.'

'So how did he die?'

'He can't have died. All I did was clout him.'

'How hard?'

'How hard would you clout somebody that tried to kill you? Bliddy hard. Bliddy wallop. Down he goes and off I run. Poor Jimmy.'

He inspects the wound again.

'It looked worse but it isn't deep. A little flesh wound. I washed it at Cooper's Hole on the way up.'

'Cooper's Hole? Did you see anybody there?'

'What's that got to do with it? I saw frogs and minnows and the deep black hole, the same as always. The blood had dried and I washed it away but it made the bleeding start again. See?'

He shows how the trail of blood is slick and shining. Davie peers at the opening in the skin, the dark dried clot that has sealed it. He thinks of old Doctor Drummond leaning over Jimmy, inspecting him for wounds, finding nothing.

'It's not too deep,' says Zorro. 'But a couple of inches to the side and it could have been me heart.'

He holds his hand across his heart as if to check that it's still beating. He stands dead still and grimaces as if he's in deep pain and stares into the sky. He laughs again.

'I'm like one of them pictures in the church,' he says. 'One of them saints with arrows in them or their skin all peeled away. Or like Jesus on that massive cross beside the altar.'

Davie recalls the saints. He recalls the cross. Recalls all the images of wounds and sickness they were made to look at in church and at school. He remembers the priest's black prayer book. He digs it out of the sack and opens it and laughs at the black cover, at the black words, at what he sees and he reads aloud.

'*O Lord Jesus.*'

'Eh?' says Zorro.

'*O Lord Jesus, I adore thee hanging on the cross, wearing a crown of thorns upon thy head.*'

'Do you?'

'Aye. *And I beg thee that thy cross may free me from the deceiving angel.*'

'Aye. All right.' He peers at Davie. 'You're bonkers, aren't you?'

'Aye,' says Davie. 'Amen.'

He flings the prayer book into the air as if to make it fly and it flaps and spins and thuds down on to the earth again.

'Begone!' he cries, just as Wilf Pew did to his false leg.

He kicks it towards the fox mask and the antlers.

'Church!' says Zorro. 'Prayers! Gave up that crap years back.'

'Me too,' says Davie. 'Except for funerals.'

Zorro nods. His eyes soften. He ponders the gorse patch.

'I used to love him,' he says.

'Love who?'

'Jimmy Killen.'

He shrugs, smiles, then pauses and frowns.

'Why am I telling you this?' he says.

'I don't know,' says Davie.

'Nor do I.'

Zorro sits down, then lies on his back on the earth with his head resting on his hands.

'It was back in Mr Garner's class,' he says. 'And before that too. Nobody knew. We were supposed to hate each other's guts, like proper Killens and proper Craigs. But we couldn't do it.'

'You were friends,' says Davie.

'Aye. We used to meet each other in sunny early mornings before school. In the autumn and the winter when the days were dark we used to walk along the river together after school. I used to say if I'd been born a Killen we could be proper pals. He used to say if he'd been born a Craig we could be proper mates. You know, the kind of things you say to each other when you're just lads. The way that you mebbe still do, Davie. Do you?'

Davie thinks about Gosh. He thinks of other pals. He thinks of the wonder of wandering with a friend at dusk as the light changes and the world and your heart seem charged.

'Do you?' says Zorro again.

'Aye,' says Davie.

'Aye. Sometimes it's like you're not supposed to say such things, not if you're a lad, but you feel them, don't you? And sometimes you have to say them, don't you?'

'Aye.'

'You can't be just a hard bugger, can you?'

'No,' says Davie.

Davie looks at the older boy. For years he's thought that Zorro Craig is hard as nails. Everybody has thought that Zorro Craig is hard as nails and nothing else. But Davie knows that nobody can be just one thing, that each of us has to be many things as we wander through the world.

Zorro is silent. Davie draws him in his mind: the blue jeans, black boots, black hair, white skin, red blood.

'But then,' says Zorro, 'we got older and we did get

harder and it was like we couldn't escape what we were supposed to be. And we were seen together and it wasn't liked and one day I got beaten up by my cousins and told I had to be a proper Craig, and Jimmy got beaten up by his and told to be a proper Killen. And that's what we became. And we were stupid, and too stupid to know that we were stupid. And there came the day we had our first fight and I felt his knuckles thumping into my cheek and he felt my knee thumping into his nuts and we knew that things had changed and we'd be battling each other for ever more.'

He pauses. There are tears in his eyes.

'And now you tell me Jimmy's dead,' he says. 'And I can't believe it but mebbe I must.'

A tiny black beetle appears, crawling across Zorro's body and up towards his chest. They both watch it.

'Do you think he thinks I'm the whole world?' says Zorro. 'Do you think he thinks I'm God?' He smiles. 'Instead of being born a Craig or a Killen, I could've been born a beetle. D'you ever think that?'

Davie has. It's the kind of thought he often has. He says so, and he imagines it now, being tiny, black and shining, making his way across a great expanse of white skin towards the wound.

'We met early this morning,' says Zorro. 'We knew we were probably going to fight. We knew we probably wanted to fight. We set it up the night before. We said it was all about a lass.'

'Maria O'Flynn.'

'How do you know that?'

'I met her at the kissing gate. She's looking for you.'

'Ah. Yes, lovely Maria. We said we both loved her. We both said she loved us. But it was nowt to do with her, not really. It was to do with us. She was just the excuse for it.'

'That's what she says.'

'She says the truth.'

He pauses. He gently flicks the beetle away. The light is changing, the sun darkening to orange as it hangs lower in the western sky. Still the air is hot. Still the yellow rises from the gorse. Songbirds sing in the yellow shrubs and the bees buzz on. Davie is entranced by the words of the older boy. He needs to hear the story, to be told the brand-new ancient tale of love and death. He closes his eyes, preparing to listen as if the tale will come to him as if in a dream.

'Stand up,' says Zorro.

'What?'

'Stand up. Be Jimmy Killen.'

'What?'

'I need you to be Jimmy Killen. I need you to know truly what occurred.'

Davie doesn't move. He sits there on the rock.

'Do it,' says Zorro. 'Or I'll pull you up and pummel you without a fight.'

And he reaches down and grabs Davie by the arm and pulls him up and glares into his eyes.

'Do it!' he snarls. 'Stop being good little Davie. Be Jimmy Killen now.'

TWENTY-THREE

Zorro holds Davie by the collar. He continues to glare into his eyes. He indicates the gorse patch.

'This is the demolition site,' he says. 'This is the back of the hall. This is where we met in the early morning. Can you see it?'

'Yes,' says Davie. He's timid, he's scared, his voice is frail.

'No!' says Zorro. 'You're a Killen. Say it like a Killen. Say it like you hate my bliddy guts.'

'Yes,' says Davie again. He looks into the gorse. He tries to see the ruined hall, the demolition site. He tries to turn this place into the place that exists so far below.

'This is where we were in Mr Garner's class,' says Zorro. 'Remember, Jimmy, back when we were small? Say yes.'

'Yes,' says Davie.

'Say it harder!'

'Aye. Aye!'

'That's better. Now tell me that you hate me. Do it. You'll never understand what happened until you do it. Do it, Jimmy! Say it!'

'I bliddy hate you, Zorro Craig.'

'Good. And how does that feel? How does it feel to tell somebody that you hate them?'

Davie tries to discover how it feels. He tries to feel that it's a terrible thing to feel. He wants to say he hates nobody and nothing. He wants to tell Zorro Craig that he doesn't hate him, cannot hate him. He wants to pull away and run back home. But he's breathing hard. He's reeling. He's turning into Jimmy Killen now, and he's glaring back into Zorro's eyes, and suddenly, as the words come out of him, he knows how powerful it is to hate.

'I hate your guts,' he says in a deep strange whisper. 'I bliddy hate you, Zorro Craig.'

'Good lad. And I hate you, Jimmy Killen. I can't stand you. I want you dead. Now go for me, Jimmy. Do what you did this morning. Go for me like you want to kill.'

Davie pauses, but just for a second. Then his hatred drives him on. He lunges forward. The boys clench each other's hands. They snarl and glare and drool. Zorro is bigger and stronger but Davie doesn't relent. He won't let himself be overwhelmed, won't let Zorro push him to the ground. He's gasping. Tears pour from his eyes, snot from his nose, saliva from his mouth. His limbs shudder, his muscles ache. He doesn't think he can go on but he goes on. He wants to crush this older boy, to finish him, to kill him. His mind roars and swirls with images of his mother's tears, his father's groans, the funeral car, the coffin, the grave, with images of Paddy Kelly praying, with the sounds of the Doonans' singing. He curses, blasphemes and yells. And Zorro holds him, fights him. They stamp on each other's feet, they butt each other.

And then suddenly Zorro comes in very close and kisses Davie's cheek, so hard.

He kisses it again, so gentle.

Davie flinches. And they both pause, still in each other's grip.

'This is when you do it,' says Zorro.

Davie stares through his blurring tears.

'This is when you get the knife out,' says Zorro.

Davie can't speak.

'So get the knife out,' says Zorro. 'Try to kill me, Jimmy.'

Davie cries.

'I haven't got a knife.'

'No. But just pretend you have. Remember the knife you saw below. That's the one. Get it out and stab me.'

Davie remembers. He recalls the look of it. He reaches into his pocket and takes it out and thrusts it at Zorro's heart. And he sees the knife hit the arm and not the heart. And he feels Zorro's clout on his cheek and down he goes.

And he lies again on the earth in the gorse patch.

'So did I kill you, Jimmy?' says Zorro. 'Are you dead?'

No answer.

Davie lies there, silent, empty, all fought out.

TWENTY-FOUR

And the day continues changing. And Zorro Craig lies on the earth not far from Davie's side. He stares into the sky, maybe contemplating the immensity of what has taken place today, maybe wishing that he could go back to this morning, or back to the very start of things so that he could change those things, so that everything could start again and take a different course. And he cries, maybe for his lost enemy and friend, maybe for the loss of himself as he used to be in Mr Garner's class and in the time before, when he was small. Or maybe there's no real reason for his crying, except that it is caused by the weird ways of this weird world, the way that love can turn to hate, the way that life is overwhelmed by death and death by life, the way that light becomes the dark and dark the light. And Zorro's young, and all the joys and pain of being Zorro Craig are experienced by a young body, a young mind, a young heart and soul. And how can he come to terms with all this without shedding tears? So he lies there and cries and there's no easy explanation.

And Davie lies like Jimmy did this morning, with blood on his cheek from Zorro's clout. But there's not much pain. He feels a kind of joy, a kind of lightness. He doesn't want to move, doesn't want to stem the flow of images and memories that pour through him now as if they've been unblocked, released and allowed to flow. Simple images of moments with his dad and with his mam. Simple memories of his dad's breath on his cheek, his voice in his ear, his hand on his shoulder, his whisper: *Don't worry, son. Keep on wandering. You'll be all right.*

And he finds himself smiling at the thought of going back down again with Zorro Craig, crossing the fields, entering the town, being welcomed home.

He opens his eyes and sees Zorro lying close by.

He takes out the pencils and sketch book and draws the older boy, then draws the battle that has just been fought inside the gorse patch, draws two boys struggling with each other upon the earth, below the sky. He draws their grunts and groans and cries swirling about them, like the great swirl of starlings that has now appeared above.

'Look,' says Davie.

Zorro turns.

'Look at what?'

Davie points upward.

'At the birds.'

And they both look, and there they are, the starlings, a thousand thousand of them drawn out by the fading light, swirling points of blackness against the sky, each single bird drawn in, caught up in the astounding dance.

They watch for a while, then Zorro turns his eyes to Davie.

'Are you all right?' he says.

'Aye,' says Davie.

He rubs the sore patch on his face. He shrugs and grins.

'Aye,' he says again. 'I'm all right. But I'm famished.'

And he digs into the haversack and says,

'Do you want some bara brith?'

'What the hell's bara brith?'

'It's bread with fruit in it. Me mam makes it. There's some Cheshire cheese as well.'

'Aye. All right.'

Zorro wipes his eyes with his black shirt.

Davie unwraps the food from the greaseproof paper. It's warm and dense. The butter has melted and seeped into the bread. The cheese is soft. It all smells delicious.

He breaks it, and passes half to Zorro.

They eat in silence while the birds swirl high above.

There are a few drops of the Coca-Cola left. They share them. They finish everything. They lick their fingers. They lick their lips.

'Tell your mam,' murmurs Zorro, 'that her bara brith is delicious.'

'I will,' says Davie.

And Zorro inspects his wound and sees that it continues to heal, and he pulls his shirt back on, and Davie sighs. It's as if the whole day has been intended for this, this moment when he eats his mam's bara brith with Zorro Craig, the murderer, high above the town, among a patch of gorse.

TWENTY-FIVE

And as they leave, the air's hot and still, despite the fading light. And outside the gorse patch there's no Foulmouth and no Wilf Pew. Davie looks around. Nobody in sight.

'Did you see anybody here?' he says.

'You keep on asking did I see anybody. I saw nobody, not till you.'

'Did you see a dog?'

'The world's filled with roaming dogs, Davie. I saw one or two, like always.'

He pauses and looks northward.

'Mebbe I should be a roaming dog myself,' he says. 'Mebbe I should just go off and start a life of wandering. Mebbe we could go together, Davie. We could be vagabonds and refugees, running away from the boring world and from the long arm of the law. You fancy that?'

He laughs.

'But you've got nowt to run from, have you?'

Davie shrugs and stares into the north. It's not just crimes you run from. Part of him does ache to go with Zorro. He wants to run for freedom, for the simple joy of it. And he knows he can't just yet, not when he's so young, not when he's still got school and he's got his mam to think about, but he knows he will one day.

And then he wants to ask Zorro if he can see the dark shadow walking away across the earth, towards the open spaces of the north. It's one-legged Wilf Pew, swaying as he walks, leaning with each step on to his hawthorn crutch.

'Do you see him now?' says Davie.

But it's too late. Already Wilf is fading into the landscape, and now he's gone.

'See who?' says Zorro.

'Nobody.'

'Nobody! Yes, I see Nobody. There he is. And there, and there! The world is filled with Nobodies!'

He laughs and shakes his head.

'I won't run,' he says. 'It's pointless. They'd catch

me, wouldn't they? It's not the Wild West, is it? There's no frontier to head for, is there?'

Maybe there is, thinks Davie. *Maybe we're always heading to a frontier, even if we don't know we are.*

'And, anyway,' says Zorro. 'We've got nowt to eat nor drink, have we? We'd die of thirst or starve to death. The last things to pass our lips would be bara brith and Coca-Cola.'

Davie grins.

'Aye,' he says. 'That's just the kind of thing that happens to the hungry kids round here.'

He gets the picture of them in his mind, two dead lads lying side by side in a dried-out stream beneath the blazing sun. He'll draw that too when he gets back home. He'll draw all the ways that he's been today, and all the ways it's possible to be. He'll draw a dozen Davies, each one in a different scene, each one discovering a strange new way of being Davie.

He walks with Zorro away from the gorse patch, past the hedgerows, across the paddock with the black-and-white pony in it.

They come to the hawthorn tree with Wilf Pew's leg in it.

Zorro reaches up and raps the leg with his fist and

it gives a hollow dong sound. He raps it again like it's a drum. He shuffles his feet like he's dancing to it.

'Any clues?' he says to Davie.

Davie shrugs. It seems too crazy to tell Zorro what really occurred. He shakes his head.

'Beyond me, Zorro,' he says.

'Beyond bliddy me as well.'

They decide to leave it there. They say it'll be a good thing to get folk thinking about it and making up their tales about it.

They move on across the damaged lovely earth to the crest above their town and they look down. Everything's as it was but for the changing light. Already a few lamps are burning in distant windows. Car headlamps move on the streets and roads. The distant sea is almost black. The river shines like ink. There's a low deep humming that Davie realises is always there, a mingling of traffic and engines, birdsong and children, gossip, cries and laughter, the sound of his own heart and his own breath, all making the music of the world in which he's grown.

And there's sweet music again – singing and fiddles and the beat of a drum. And the calling of the footballers who still swarm across the field. They'll play till night, he knows, until the ball becomes a black shadow until at last, like the players themselves, it won't be seen at all.

On they move, stepping into the depression in the earth that leads to Cooper's Hole. Davie's nervous, his breath and heart quicken, but there's nothing. Just the water, the weeds, the low trees, the tender turf, the hole itself. The hole seems larger now, darker, it seems to be breathing out darkness into the world as the gorse patch seemed to breathe out light.

The sound of the splashing water draws them to it.

'This is one of the places we used to come,' says Zorro.

'You and Jimmy?'

'Aye. We used to say that nobody would find us here. And they didn't. Nobody ever found us. It's weird. Hardly anybody seems to know about this place.'

'I know,' says Davie. 'Yes, it's weird, eh?'

'We used to talk about the days when we'd be free, when we'd be able to forget all the stupid nonsense about our families and all the stupid nonsense that's in this place. We talked about travelling away together. We used to say it wouldn't be long till freedom came.'

Zorro crouches down, cups his hands and drinks.

'Ha! And now look how it's all turned out.'

He drinks again.

'And we told each other we saw ghosts up here.'

'Ghosts?'

'Aye. Lads from the pits from times before.'

'I've seen them as well,' says Davie.

'Aye?' says Zorro, unsurprised.

Davie cups his hands and drinks.

'They say,' he says, 'that drinking the water here brings you visions.'

'Jimmy used to say that. You believe it?'

'I dunno. I sometimes think we can see anything no matter what we drink.'

'If your mind starts wandering, eh? If your imagination gets to work.'

'Aye.'

There are noises in the shrubs and undergrowth: rabbits, rats, roosting birds. A frog plops into the water. They see its kicking legs, its gleaming back, its widening wake that catches the light.

'That's beautiful,' says Zorro.

'Aye. It is.'

'We could have been like them, couldn't we?'

'Like the frogs?'

'Ha! No. Like the pit lads, Davie.'

'If we'd been born a hundred years before.'

'And what if we'd been born a thousand years before? Ten thousand years before?'

'Living in huts. Living in caves.'

'Running across the world with spears, hunting.'

'Oh, I'd have fancied that!'

Zorro dreams of chasing beasts across the land. Davie dreams of being in a cave beneath. He stands before the cave wall, painting. He makes marks on the wall like he makes marks in his sketch book. There's a Davie way back then and a Davie here right now. Both Davies make the marks that link the present and the past.

'It's all chance, isn't it?' he says. 'The time we're born, where we're born, who we're born to.'

'And I suppose we could have been like frogs as well.'

'Or even like the grass.'

'Or like the water.'

'Or the sky.'

And they smile at the thought of being water and sky, and around them in the shadows the ghosts start rising, boys like them come out from below, come out from the ancient darkness. Davie and Zorro stay still, and say nothing until the moment fades and the ghosts are gone.

'See them?' says Zorro.

'Aye,' says Davie.

'Ghosts of how we might have been.'

'And mebbe we're like ghosts to them.'

'Aye,' says Zorro.

Davie pauses. He wants the other ghost to rise, the other memory. Nothing comes.

So he murmurs, 'Let's go on.'

Then there's a snuffling, and he knows it's the dog, Foulmouth, somewhere nearby.

He sighs.

'Go away,' he mutters, under his breath.

He sees it, coming through the shadows.

Then a voice.

'Zorro? Zorro, are you there?'

Zorro gasps.

They see the boy behind the dog.

'Zorro, is that you?'

And they see that it's the dead lad, Jimmy Killen, coming towards them through the shades.

TWENTY-SIX

Zorro and Davie don't move, can't move.

Jimmy keeps on slowly coming.

'You're dead,' says Zorro.

It's Jimmy. His face, his body. The green checky Levi shirt with blood on it, the jeans, black winklepicker boots.

'Jimmy,' says Zorro, 'you're bliddy dead.'

Jimmy grins. His grin.

'Who telt you that?' he says.

His voice, the voice of Jimmy Killen.

Zorro's trembling. His voice is quaking.

'This lad here,' he says. 'His name is Davie.'

Jimmy grins again.

'You're not alone,' he says. 'That was the tale that many telt.'

'But I saw you,' says Davie.

He wants to scream, he wants to run, this can't be true.

'And that's what many saw,' says Jimmy. 'But touch me. Go on. Touch me.'

He raises his hands, offering them to the two boys.

'Touch,' he says again. 'I'm living flesh and blood.'

But Zorro and Davie can't reach out, can't try to touch.

So Jimmy comes in closer and he raises his hands higher and grips each of them by the shoulder.

Davie gasps. Real hands, real bones, real muscle, flesh and skin.

And the smell of the boy, and the heat coming from him, and the shining of his eyes.

'See?' says Jimmy. 'It's me, Jimmy Killen, alive, not dead.'

He crouches down, cups his hands under the falling water and he drinks.

'I thought of you here, Zorro,' he says. 'I thought you might be here. I telt them I want to find Zorro and they said you can't, you're not strong enough yet. Then this dog come, like it had come seeking me, and I said I had to go and I let it lead me here.'

He drinks again.

'I think there's a few not far behind,' he says. 'They're worried about me, that I might fall again. I heard them following.'

He turns around. Nobody in sight.

'You were dead,' says Davie.

'It was that daft old doctor,' says Jimmy. 'It was that daft old priest. Two old blokes that should be specialists in death that can't even tell if a lad is dead or still alive.'

'You weren't dead?' says Davie.

'I was flat out, knocked out. It took me a while to come around.' He laughs. 'You clouted me good and hard, eh, Zorro?'

'Only 'cos you stabbed me.'

'It was the lass in the ambulance that telt them. "Get out the way," she said. "This lad isn't dead." When I came round it was her face I seen, in the hospital. "Hello, Jimmy," she said. "Welcome back."'

He giggles like a child and spreads his arms wide in delight.

'I'm not a ghost,' he says. 'I'm resurrected like the Lord!'

The dog snuffles and drools.

'Good dog,' says Jimmy.

He reaches out and strokes its head.

'You led me to the right place, lad,' he says.

The dog stands up and stretches and yawns like it needs to sleep, then it pads away from them.

'It's an ugly bugger,' whispers Jimmy. 'Isn't it?'

'Aye,' says Davie. 'It's called Foulmouth.'

'I know where it got that name from!' says Jimmy.

They watch it go, heading back towards the crest.

Then the three of them just stand together at Cooper's Hole, as if they're lost, as if they're little boys that need somebody to tell them what to do. And they don't look at each other, like they can't look at each other, and they look at the water, the earth, the sky, anywhere but at each other. Then Zorro lets out a string of curses that are filled with astonishment, terror and delight. And he says that he supposes they should all just go back down again. And Jimmy says that he supposes that they should as well. He says that there was talk of some kind of party happening in the field below and they should make their way to it.

And then he just gasps and he says,

'Oh, Zorro, come here, Zorro!'

And the two boys put their arms around each other and hold each other tight.

TWENTY-SEVEN

Davie leads them away from Cooper's Hole across the uneven, beautiful and damaged earth, past knocked-down terraced houses and ancient broken garden walls, past boarded-over and fenced-off pit-shafts, past turfed pit-heaps and ripped-up rail lines, and as they approach the kissing gate he feels a touch on his shoulder, breath on his cheek, and he slows for a moment, just time enough to whisper, 'Goodbye,' and then he moves on.

And the day quickens in its fading. At the edges of Davie's vision there are the silhouettes of deer. And there are early bats as well as starlings flickering in the sky. And still the skylarks sing.

Maria O'Flynn is at the gate. She kisses Davie as he steps through and she waits there for the other two boys. He doesn't pause. He hears her crying as she greets them.

The group beyond the gate is made up of Killens and Craigs, of curious kids, of wonderers.

He sees Anthony Killen, the man he met on the way up.

'Did the battle start?' Davie asks him.

Anthony laughs.

'We were up for it. We glared and stamped and the knives were out. We were all about to start. Then a lad came running up, yelling the truth about Jimmy's death, so there was no way for us to go on. Many were disappointed, of course. There's some that always want the war.'

He stares over Davie's shoulder.

'And here comes the truth behind it all,' he says. 'Who'd have thought it? Jimmy Killen back in the world again.'

He shakes his head in wonder.

'Mebbe we all need a death and resurrection,' he says, 'to bring us to our senses. What do you think, son?'

Davie says he doesn't know.

He carries on.

He wonders how it might feel to be resurrected, to be turned to nothing and then back into something again. He tries to imagine total darkness, total absence. He tries to imagine death, but there's no way to do that, not when the body thrives, the senses reel, the heart beats, the mind roams and the soul soars. So there's no way of knowing how resurrection might feel. He only knows that he's alive. His heart beats. He breathes. He's made of skin and flesh and bone. His feet carry him onward, downward. He feels the ease of his body, this thing of many parts that move in harmony. He knows the beauty of being a living thing and of being part of everything around. He tastes the dusk and smells the dusk and the dusk enters him and becomes part of him. A fox calls, from not far away, and the call enters through the ear and becomes part of him. The first billion-miles-away stars already shine in the sky and they enter through these eyes and become part of him. The dust in the dusk becomes part of him. The scent of grass becomes part of him. The sound of distant children calling becomes part of him. The starlings swirl in him. The fox prowls in him. It all becomes part of this kid, this lad, this boy-becoming-man, this ordinary fragment of the ordinary world. He moves downward through the Tyneside dusk and in the fading light the everyday miracle occurs as he blurs and becomes all things and all things become this troubled, joyous, ordinary, yearning boy named Davie.

And, 'Davie! Davie!' comes a call from down below and here comes another boy running upward, and it's the boy he met at the start of the tale, his friend Gosh Todd.

'Davie!' gasps Gosh. 'Where you been?'

'Just wandering,' says Davie.

'Wandering! You missed it all.'

'Did I?'

'Aye. Jimmy Killen, Davie! He wasn't even bliddy dead!'

Davie laughs.

He pauses and looks back. He sees the shadowy bodies of Jimmy and Zorro descending. He sees their followers, their friends, their admirers, those lost in amazement and puzzlement. He looks down. Many folk are already gathered on the field above the allotments. Music is being played. A fire is flickering to life. Should he wait here with Gosh and let those behind catch up? Should he descend the final stretch of the hill with the murderer who's no longer a murderer and the dead lad who's no longer dead? Should he be with them when they're welcomed back? Should he share the excitement, the acclaim?

No. He starts to run down the zigzag path with the haversack bouncing at his back, and Gosh runs too, and they run through the drift of dark red poppies and they run on to the grass of the dark green field and through a bunch of yelling kids still playing the everlasting game and they run to the fire and they fling themselves on to the grass beside it and someone puts a sausage sandwich into each of their hands and they laugh and start to eat and Davie looks up and there above them is Letitia Spall with her hands on her hips and the dusk reflected in her deep dark eyes and she tousles Davie's hair and she says, 'Well, look what the buzzard has brought back to us. Is this the same babe? Or have you been carried back by a different buzzard and you're a different babe?'

TWENTY-EIGHT

Is he a different babe, a different Davie?

Letitia smiles at him as he wonders about the question, and for a moment all kinds of Davies wander and swarm and fly through him like birds and beasts and dreams.

But then he shakes such images from his head and he laughs.

'No,' he tells her. 'I was carried back by the same buzzard. I'm the same babe . . . I think so, anyway, Mrs Spall.'

Gosh stares at the two of them.

'What the hell you on about?' he says.

'And are you the same Gosh,' says Davie, 'that I was with this morning?'

'What?' says Gosh.

Letitia laughs and turns away.

Davie bites the delicious sandwich.

'And do you think a sausage once had a soul?' says Davie.

'What?' says Gosh.

'And do you ever think you might be a beetle?'

Gosh groans and taps his temple.

'You always were a bit,' he says.

'A bit what?'

'A bit mental, man.'

They giggle at each other then they lunge at each other and fight like they have done ever since they were small. They wrestle and roll and snort and laugh and then Gosh gets the upper hand and he sits on Davie's chest, pressing Davie's arms down with his knees. Davie feels the hard pencil case pressing into his back.

'Beg for mercy, you worm,' Gosh says, just like he used to when they were small.

'Na!'

Gosh glares.

'Submit. Give up.'

'Na!'

'I'm ganna have to kill you, then.'

'Gan on then. See if I care.'

Gosh draws his fist back and glares, about to strike,

but just in time Davie throws him off and they wrestle again until they're in a clinch.

'Squits?' says Gosh.

'Aye,' says Davie. 'Squits.'

They roll apart and lie on the grass and stare at the sky.

'I've lost me sandwich,' says Gosh.

'Me too.'

Somebody heard. Straight away somebody's asking,

'Would you like another sausage sandwich?'

Davie looks up and Catherine and Lara are there. Catherine is holding out two sandwiches. Lara is holding out two bowls.

'Hello, Mr Nit,' the girls say together.

Davie laughs.

'Hello,' he says. 'How's the garden getting on?'

'Very well indeed,' say the girls together.

'We've taken a break,' says Catherine. 'Mam says it's just as important to feed the people in the real world.'

'It is!' says Davie.

He takes a sandwich.

'Would you like to dip it in some sauce?' says Lara. She holds the bowls towards him.

'You can have red or brown,' she says.

'Can I have a bit of both?'

She shakes her head.

'No, it mixes the colours and the tastes up and people don't like it.'

'I could dip one end of the sandwich in brown and the other in red,' he says.

She ponders.

'You could,' she says. 'But be very careful not to mix them up or there'll be trouble.'

Davie does as she says.

Gosh dips his sandwich in the red.

'Are you a nit as well?' says Catherine.

'No!' says Gosh.

'If he's not a nit,' says Lara, 'then he must be a dafty.'

Gosh laughs and bites his sandwich.

'How's that monster getting on?' says Davie.

'He is still,' says Lara, staring intently at Davie, 'waiting for his chance.'

'But the fairies, you will be pleased to know,' says Catherine, 'are doing very well indeed.'

'That's good,' says Davie.

'Of course it is!' says Lara. 'Everybody knows that!'

'And we can't stand here gossiping all night,' says

Catherine. 'There are people to feed, you know!'

They turn away.

'Bye bye, Mr Nit,' they say together. 'Bye bye, Mr Dafty.'

Gosh groans. Maybe he wants to ask what that was all about but he doesn't. He just says he's glad he got another sandwich.

All around them, people continue to gather, wanderers from the town below, footballers detaching themselves from the game, couples and families and little groups. The day's still darkening, the fire's burning higher, glowing brighter, a fragment of the sun down here on earth.

'Look at them two,' says Gosh.

Davie looks, and there are Doctor Drummond and Father Noone strolling side by side in deep conversation.

Gosh laughs.

'You'd think two buggers like that would know if somebody's dead or not, wouldn't you?' he says.

'Aye,' says Davie. 'You certainly would.'

The music comes to life. Musicians at the edge of the light. The Doonans, with their fiddles and drums and whistles and pipes, and others start gathering around them. There are kids with recorders and kazoos. An old bloke plays a comb across his mouth. Another taps spoons on his thigh. People whistle and hum, gently clap their hands and gently stamp their feet. It isn't raucous yet, but calm, shifting, reflective, as if it's part of the changing light. Shona sings and her voice rises with the sparks from the fire towards the first few stars.

The dark keeps coming on.

The Killens and the Craigs are gathering. They'd have been at war today if Jimmy had been really dead. But now the children are children, running together, wrestling, sitting in little serious groups. The adults have relaxed. Their movements aren't stiff and muscly, but are fluid, more gentle. Their voices are softer. Maybe they don't feel the old need to strike the old warlike gestures now that the light has diminished and the kinder aspects of their bodies and their souls can be shown.

The football game is nearly over. Nearly too dark to see the ball. Even as the daylight fades, the starlings still swirl in the sky and then they swarm down to the earth again and then they're gone. The bats are flickering. There's dancing and love everywhere. Fernando Craig and a bonny lass, Letitia and Annie, Lara and Catherine. Is that two men who dance half-secretly together in the deeper darkness?

There's sudden applause, a gentle roar as Jimmy Killen and Zorro Craig appear by the fire with Maria between them.

Gosh jumps up at that.

'It's them!' he says. 'Davie, howay!'

Davie holds back and Gosh shakes his head and hurries to the supposed murderer and his victim. Others hurry with him, to call out their astonishment and delight at what seems to have occurred today.

Davie's mam comes to his side.

She ruffles his hair.

'Hello, stranger,' she says.

'Hello, Mam.'

'And where did you get to?'

'Oh, you know. Just went off on a wander.'

'Like always, eh? That's good.'

Davie ponders. He knows he'll tell her about what he saw at Cooper's Hole today, but he'll wait for a proper time for that. He'll open his book and show her the pictures he's made. He'll make other pictures, drawing the images from his mind and allowing them to live again on his pages. And he'll use them to recreate the whole day, and to help him explain what he's seen and what he's been through.

He smiles, realising that he might be recreating this day in pictures and in words for the rest of his life.

They watch the folk around Jimmy and Zorro.

'It's strange,' says Mam. 'When I found out about the murder, I tried being dead worried about you. But I kind of knew it would all be nowt. I knew you'd be OK, that we'd all be OK.'

'And it is. And we are.'

She kisses his brow.

'The worst's over, son,' she whispers.

He leans into her and they breathe and sway together to the music. The Doonans play some of the same music and sing some of the same songs that they sang at the funeral, but with different rhythms, different tones, and the music that lamented death becomes a music that announces life.

Davie starts to lose himself in it, and in his mother and in his ever-moving mind.

'The bara brith was lovely,' he murmurs softly.

'I'm glad to hear it.'

Then there's a man at their side. It's Oliver

Henderson, from the allotments, still in his gardener's clothes.

'Could I have the next dance, ma'am?' he says.

Davie's mam giggles.

'Certainly, Mr Henderson,' she says.

She winks at her son and steps away and Mr Henderson leads her in a very formal-looking, rather stately dance, moving through the flickering shadows, the flickering light.

Davie stands alone for a while, in this field full of folk halfway between the town and sky.

Then Shona is with him. They smile at each other and greet each other but they don't say much. They wander away. Davie finds her hand in his. They pause and look back to the beautiful fire with the sparks spiralling through the darkness. They listen to the music. They see the silhouettes of deer and a fox nearby. They hear the hooting of an owl and then there comes a voice, just as it did the morning.

'Now then, Davie.'

It's Paddy Kelly. He's standing with his face towards the fire and it's shining bright. He is in his blue T-shirt. No black on his body, no white collar at his neck. A dark-haired woman is at his side.

'Now then, Paddy,' Davie replies.

'You'll see I cast the blackness off.'

'I do, Paddy.'

'I've come back to life, just like the dead lad did. So now I make my new way through the world.'

The woman shyly lifts her face and smiles.

'As do you, Davie,' says Paddy. 'As do we all. Good evening to you, Shona Doonan.'

'Good evening, Father.'

'Ah, no, that's all done. It's simple Paddy now.'

The woman takes his hand. They dance. They step away.

Davie scans the place they've come from.

'What you looking for?' says Shona.

'I thought Wilf Pew might come down to join in with everything.'

'Ah, the poor man.'

'Poor man?'

'You didn't hear?'

'No.'

'Found passed away in his flat yesterday morning.'

Davie says nothing.

'He scared me stiff when I was little,' says Shona. 'But he was a canny man.'

Davie reels and then composes himself. He says nothing. This is something else he'll have to find the proper time and place to think about and say.

'Davie,' Shona whispers. 'Stop thinking so much.'

She sings gently into his ear, so gently that only he can hear.

Then they wander on across the field, hand in hand, as so many young folk from this little place have done and will forever do. And as they walk, the ancient brand-new earth keeps turning, deepening the dark, bringing the lost light back to us again.